The First Time Ever Published!

The Seventh Classic Diner Mystery

From *New York Times* Bestselling Author

Jessica Beck

A BURNED OUT BAKER

Other Books by Jessica Beck

The Donut Shop Mysteries

Glazed Murder
Fatally Frosted
Sinister Sprinkles
Evil Éclairs
Tragic Toppings
Killer Crullers
Drop Dead Chocolate
Powdered Peril
Illegally Iced
Deadly Donuts
Assault and Batter
Sweet Suspects

The Classic Diner Mysteries

A Chili Death
A Deadly Beef
A Killer Cake
A Baked Ham
A Bad Egg
A Real Pickle
A Burned Out Baker

The Ghost Cat Cozy Mysteries

Ghost Cat: Midnight Paws
Ghost Cat 2: Bid for Midnight

Jessica Beck is the *New York Times* Bestselling Author of the Donut Mysteries, the Classic Diner Mysteries, and the Ghost Cat Cozy Mysteries.

To Agatha Christie, Charlotte MacLeod, and Carolyn Hart, three ladies who started me on this lovely journey with their wonderful books that inspired me to try!

Chapter 1

"Moose, I'm not going to stand for this! You might not like what I'm doing, but there's nothing you can do to stop me!"

I glanced up from the table I was serving to see Barry Jackson, a heavyset balding man in his late thirties, yelling. Why on earth was he shouting at my grandfather? That was unacceptable behavior coming from the baker, and not just because Moose and I were family. Barry was yelling at him in The Charming Moose Diner, my grandfather's namesake and the business I now ran myself, along with lots of help from my husband, my mother, and at times, my grandmother, as well as Moose himself.

"Barry, you need to simmer down and watch your tone of voice with me," my grandfather said in a controlled manner. I could see that he was fighting his own temper, and I wondered how long it would take for him to give in to it.

Knowing Moose, it wouldn't be long.

Barry took a deep breath, and then he wiped his brow with his ever-present handkerchief. Though his face was still beet red, at least he wasn't throwing punches.

Yet.

I decided that it was time to act before things escalated more than they already had.

I left my customers and approached Barry, putting myself between him and my grandfather. "What's going on here?"

Before the baker could answer, my husband, Greg, came out of the back where he'd been cleaning up for the night. "Is everything all right out here, Victoria?" he asked. "I heard shouting."

"It's going to be," I said confidently. "I'm handling it."

"Call me if you need me," Greg said, and then he quickly disappeared back into the kitchen. That was one of the many things I loved about my husband. He knew that when we were at The Charming Moose, I was in charge, and he fully respected it.

"I promise," I said, and after he was gone, I turned back to the baker. "Now, take a deep breath and tell me why you are so upset, Barry."

"Don't try to use that reasonable tone of voice with *me*, Victoria," Barry snapped. "I'm pretty sure that you put your grandfather up to it, so don't even try to deny it."

I looked at Moose. "Do you have any idea what he's talking about?"

"I don't have a clue," my grandfather said a little testily, "but if he doesn't develop some better manners, and I mean fast, I'm throwing him out on his ear."

"Let's at least wait and hear what he has to say first," I said, doing my best to appease my grandfather. I was his biggest fan, but the man had a bite that was actually worse than his bark, and nobody in the diner needed to see him lose his temper with Barry.

"Fine, but he'd better do a good job of explaining himself. I don't appreciate being attacked in my, er, your diner, Victoria."

"Then you know exactly how I feel," Barry said petulantly. "When I bought Iced from Francie Humphries and changed the name to Flour Power, I swore that I'd make it a success, and I'm determined to do it, no matter how hard you try to stop me."

"Enough with the drama, Barry. Just tell us what's going on," I said. I was losing my patience with the man myself, so I couldn't even begin to imagine how Moose must be feeling.

"This says it all," he said triumphantly as he pulled a torn flyer out of his apron pocket and jammed it into my face.

"Let me see that," I said as I pulled it from his clutching fingers. Barry Jackson had sausages for digits, and I wondered how he made some of the delicate pastries he produced in his bakery.

In a bold font, the flyer proclaimed, "Jacob's Fork, Now You Can All Have The Breakfast You Deserve!!!"

Below that, the text read, "Flour Power is proud to announce that as of right now, we are offering a far better alternative to what's been available for breakfast in town up until now. We are serving biscuits of all kinds for breakfast at the bakery, and we guarantee that you won't be disappointed!!! Bring in a receipt from The Charming Moose for breakfast and get a free biscuit. If it's not the best thing you ever tasted, we'll give you another one, but one bite is all that it's going to take!!!"

"What do you say to that?" Barry asked me with a smirk.

I frowned at the flyer in my hand. "I do have one question. If they don't like the first biscuit, why would they want another one, whether it's free or not?"

"Give that back to me. It doesn't say that at all," he said as he yanked it out of my hand, tearing it again.

The edge still in my hand fluttered to the floor as I released it. "As a matter of fact, it does, but I'm not going to argue with you about it. It still doesn't explain why you are standing in my diner yelling at Moose."

"He tore down every flyer I put up in town!" Barry said, his face reddening even more.

"That's a straight-out lie," Moose said, his voice turning into a growl.

This was starting to get ugly fast. "Gentlemen, let's take this outside," I said as I looked around the diner and noticed all the gazes centered on us. We had quite an audience, even though it was nearly closing time. I personally didn't know how these folks could eat dinner at seven at night, but then again, I doubted many of them got to work at six AM like I did.

"You can't throw me out!" Barry said. "I have as much a right to be here as anyone else."

"Think again after you read the sign," Moose said as he pointed to the sign under the register that reserved that exact right for us. It had saved me more than once during my time running the diner, and I was glad that Moose had started the tradition soon after opening the place all those years ago.

"Take it easy. Nobody's throwing you out, Barry," I said as calmly as I could muster. "I just think we could have a more civilized conversation without an audience."

"What are you afraid to say in front of your customers, Victoria?" he asked accusingly. "What are you trying to hide?"

"Nothing, you nitwit," I said, letting my temper slip out a little. "I'm just trying to keep you from making any more of a horse's hind end of yourself than you already have."

"Trust me, that ship has sailed," Moose said as he put one of his own beefy hands on the baker's shoulder. My grandfather, though a man of a certain age, was still strong and quite virile. I think it must have surprised Barry just how strong Moose really was, because he stumbled a little under my grandfather's grasp. I reached out to steady him, but he kept sinking until he was on the floor.

"They both pushed me down!" he shouted out overdramatically. "Ow, my back. Somebody call an ambulance."

"Get up, you big faker," Moose said as he towered over Barry. He started to reach down and grab the baker when I pulled my grandfather back. He looked at me with a puzzled expression. "Why are you stopping me, Victoria?"

"Moose, we can't afford a lawsuit," I said softly to him. "The premiums on our insurance policy are just about enough to put us out of business as it is. Call 911."

"But he's faking," Moose protested, and then he looked wildly around the room. "You all saw what he did, didn't you?"

There were a few nods from the crowd, but several folks avoided all eye contact with my grandfather and me.

It appeared that we might be in trouble after all.

Moose didn't move, so I pulled out my phone and dialed 911 myself. After the dispatcher came on, I said, "It's probably nothing, but we need an ambulance at The Charming Moose," I said.

"Victoria, is that you?" a woman's voice I instantly

recognized asked me.

"Hey, Karen. Yeah, somebody at the diner claims he's hurt."

"Is he just trying to get out of paying his check?" she asked.

"It's a little more than that, I'm afraid," I said.

"I'll send someone over right now," Karen said, and then she hung up.

"They're on their way," I said to Moose more than Barry.

"I don't know why you even bothered calling them, Victoria," Moose snorted as he stared down at the baker.

"You both pushed me down," Barry repeated, as though he were out of any fresh ideas.

"Keep saying it, baker man, and somebody might actually believe you eventually," Moose said.

I decided that it was time to clear out the restaurant. The last thing we needed was for our patrons to see Barry loaded up on a stretcher and taken away. "Folks, sorry about the disturbance," I said as I turned to our diners. "Tonight's meal is on the house, but I'm afraid that we're going to have to close the place early." It was three minutes until seven and they were all getting a free meal out of us, but I still knew that there would be complaints, and there were indeed a few grumbles from the diners. "Go and have a good night."

Everyone reluctantly left the diner, and the three of us were soon alone in the dining room. Greg hadn't shown himself since he'd popped out the first time, much to his credit.

"Barry, do you honestly believe that I care enough about anything that you do to go around town tearing down your flyers?" Moose asked in a soft voice.

"I'm going to put you out of business, and you know it," Barry said as he lay there. "Breakfast is just the beginning. I've got an investor with deep pockets, and we're going to expand the shop until we're three times as big as you are." He waved his hand around the room, and then he added, "For what just happened to me, I'm going to sue the pants off of all of you. Moose, it's going to give me great joy to take this place away from you, and then I'm going to laugh when they bulldoze it to the ground."

"That's never going to happen," Moose said, but I didn't like the hint of uncertainty in his voice when he said it. As the door to the diner opened, my grandfather added, "We'll see you dead before we allow that to happen."

We were all spared from hearing Barry's reply to that comment when two paramedics knelt down and started examining him. Had they heard Moose's last threat? I honestly hadn't been paying attention. I was more than a little disgusted as they took great care to load Barry onto the gurney, though I realized that it wasn't their fault. I knew that we hadn't done anything to the baker, but it might be tough to prove. The two paramedics had just loaded the stretcher into the ambulance and driven away when Sheriff Croft came in.

Needless to say, I was not pleased to see him.

"Where did everybody go?" was the first thing he asked us as he looked around the empty diner.

"*Everybody*? Exactly who were you expecting to find here?" I asked.

"The eyewitnesses," he said.

"Eyewitnesses to what?" I asked him. "There were several folks here earlier having a late dinner, but I sent them all home."

"There was nothing for anyone to see here anyway," Moose said.

"That's not the way I heard it. I got a call from one of the folks who was here saying that you two accosted Barry Jackson," he said. "Supposedly, you both knocked him to the floor."

"That's a load of manure, and you know it," Moose said.

"That's not for me to say, at least not right now," the sheriff said as he turned to me. "Victoria, I need the names of everyone who was just here. Can you do that for me?"

"Sheriff, Barry came in here yelling from the start," I

explained. "When Moose and I tried to ease him outside so we could discuss his complaint with us in private, he slipped down to the floor of his own accord."

"If you ask me, I think he planned the entire thing from the start," Moose said, not helping matters any.

"Maybe so, but I still need those names," Sheriff Croft said.

"I'll do it right now," I said as I pulled out my order pad and started jotting down the names of our previous diners. In my mind, I went from table to table, remembering the meals I'd served better than the folks who'd been eating them, but in the end, I named all but two single diners.

"There were two others I didn't know," I said.

He frowned at the list. "Were they at least together?"

"No, they were both flying solo," I said.

"That's just great," Sheriff Croft said.

"Sorry, but we don't ask for identification when people sit down to eat here," Moose said.

"That's why I was kind of hoping that no one had left yet," the sheriff said. He took my list, folded it once, and then he stuck it in his shirt pocket. "Now, do you two want to tell me your side of the story?"

"Finally," Moose said, and then we both started bringing the sheriff up to date on what had happened, and why.

"It's not true, is it?" the sheriff asked when Moose got to the part about him supposedly tearing flyers down all over town.

"Of course it's true," he said sarcastically. "I did it all on my bicycle, and they're still in the wicker basket hanging from my handlebars. What a ridiculous question."

The sheriff shrugged. "I have to ask."

"For the record, I didn't even know about Barry's new breakfast operation until he stormed in here less than half an hour ago," Moose said.

"And you?" he asked me.

"I hadn't heard one word about it," I answered.

"Okay, now, tell me about his fall."

"I told you before. He didn't fall," Moose said loudly.

"Just tell me what happened," Sheriff Croft said.

My grandfather and I told our side of the story, and the sheriff took notes in his little notebook. After we were finished, he tucked it back into his shirt pocket and said, "I'll be back in the morning."

"Where are you going now?" I asked.

"I have to track down this witness list," he said, and before Moose and I could protest any more, he was gone.

"Do you think he believes us?" I asked my grandfather after I locked the front door.

"Who knows? I'm not even sure that it matters, really. Once he talks to the people who saw what really happened, we'll be in the clear."

"I hope you're right," I said.

"What makes you say it that way, Victoria?" he asked.

"Somebody called him in the first place, remember?"

Moose frowned at that, and then he left the diner, promising to return the next day.

Greg and I finished our cleanup and had a quick dinner at home, but neither one of us was much in the mood for conversation. Barry had managed to put a pall over the whole evening, and by the time I went to bed later that night, I had visions of losing the diner forever through no fault of our own. It was the true definition of a nightmare, because I had no idea what I would do without The Charming Moose in my life. I'd done a few other things over the years, but once I'd taken over the helm from my father after his brief tenure, I knew that I had finally found exactly what it was that I'd been meant to do with my life.

And now someone was trying to take it away from me.

I was still tired when I woke up the next morning after battling the baker and his legal minions all night long in my sleep.

It was going to be a bad day; that was certain.

I just didn't know quite how bad just yet, but I'd find out soon enough.

Chapter 2

"Victoria, do you smell smoke?" my mother asked me the next morning as I unlocked the front door of The Charming Moose. It was five thirty AM, too early for any reasonable person to be at work, and yet here we were. The cold air had a bite to it, and I knew that the sun wouldn't be up for hours yet to warm it up any. I loved the chillier months, but sometimes the combination of cold and darkness got to me. Those folks who lived farther north of me had my sympathy indeed.

"Someone's probably just burning a fire in their woodstove," I said absently.

"That's not smoke from wood alone," Mom said somberly.

I forgot about the key and took in another whiff of the air. She was right. This was something more than the simple notes of wood being consumed. There were other odors mixed in as well, and I suddenly knew where I'd sampled that smell before.

"Somebody's house is on fire," I said just as the first siren filled the dark morning air.

That's when I saw the first flames leap up into the sky.

It was close to the diner, too, much closer than I liked.

Mom must have reached the same conclusion as I had as she pointed down the street. "Victoria, unless I'm mistaken, that's coming from Flour Power. Barry Jackson's bakery is on fire."

As we got closer to the fire, I knew that she was right, no matter how much I hoped that it might be otherwise. Both of the town's fire trucks were there by the time we walked over to the bakery. Flames licked the sky as the building became engulfed in ferocious flames, consuming everything, leaving nothing untouched. The men and women fighting back with their hoses tried their best, but it was clear from the start that it was a losing battle. By the time they were finished, there would be nothing left of the place that hadn't been touched by both flame and water.

The baker was, for all intents and purposes, out of business for good.

That's when I realized that something else was wrong.

"Where's Barry?" I asked as I looked around at the folks gathered to witness the inferno in hushed silence. "He should be here, shouldn't he?"

"Maybe he's still in the hospital after last night," Mom suggested.

Even though it might mean losing The Charming Moose forever, I hoped that she was right, because if Barry had been inside when that blaze started, I couldn't imagine him ever making it back out again alive.

"There's the fire chief," I told my mother as I pointed in his direction. "Let's go ask him."

"We shouldn't bother him right now, Victoria. He's busy."

I looked at the chief again, and all I could see was him standing there idly watching the streams of water hit the flames. He wasn't exactly manning a hose himself.

"This will just take a second," I said as I approached him. I noticed that my mom was right behind me, so she had to be curious, too.

We didn't make it, though, at least not right away.

"Some fire, isn't it?" Rob Bester said to me as we walked past him.

"Hey, Rob. I didn't see you standing there," I said. Rob owned the tire store next door to the bakery, and it didn't surprise me to find him out there.

"I got a call that Flour Power was on fire and that I might be next," Rob said in the dark reflected light of the flames. "It looks like they might be able to save my place. It's a shame about Barry's, though."

"It is," I said. "Listen, we have to go talk to Luke Yates. We'll talk to you later."

"Sure, go on. I'm just going to be standing right here all morning. If I have to, I'll get my hose out and help them myself."

"Hopefully it won't come to that," I said.

"You're right about that. If they need me as a volunteer, they're already in trouble."

"Hi, Luke," I said as my mother and I finally approached the fire chief.

Luke Yates nodded to me absently, his gaze still riveted on the fire. "Hello, Victoria." He spotted my mother, and then he tipped his hat to her. "Hey, Melinda. It's a real shame, isn't it?"

"It's tragic," I said as we all stared at the roaring fire. The water was finally starting to make a little headway, but there were still plenty of flames springing up from what was once our town's bakery. "Was anyone inside?"

"I sure hope not," he said, his voice filled with weariness. "But it will probably be hours before we find out."

"Why so long?"

"Things will still be hot in there for a long time, even after we extinguish the flames, which is questionable at the moment. We've already evacuated the block, and if things don't get better fast, we might have to shut you down, too."

I hadn't even considered that possibility. "But we're three blocks away from here."

The chief looked at the nearby trees dotting the street, and my gaze followed his. They were beginning to sway some in the breeze. "A wind is coming on, and if it hits, there's no telling what this is going to do. We've got calls in to four neighboring fire stations to help out. I just hope they all get here in time."

"Is there anything we can do?" my mother asked softly.

"Well, I wouldn't say no to a cup of coffee," the chief said.

"We'll take care of it, and some biscuits, too," my mother said.

"That would be much appreciated," he replied with the hint of a smile, and then we all heard sirens approaching from behind us. "That'll be some of our friends," he said with a slight smile.

"We'll get out of your way," I said. "Expect the coffee and food in half an hour."

"We'll be counting on it," he said.

Mom and I headed back to The Charming Moose, and as we walked, she asked, "You don't mind that I promised them free food and coffee, do you?"

"Of course not," I said. "I would have done it myself, but you beat me to it."

"I didn't want to speak out of turn," she said. "After all, you're the one running the diner these days."

"Don't worry about it. After all, it's a family thing," I said.

"Maybe so, but you're the one who is in charge. Moose had his turn, and so did your father. I'm quite proud of the way you've taken over. I haven't told you that lately, have I?"

The compliment warmed me more than all of the coffee in the world could have. "Thanks, I appreciate that. It's not always easy, but I love doing it."

"I can't imagine why it would be," she said with a laugh. "Still, you manage to rise to the top of every occasion."

"I'd like to think so," I said as we got to the diner and went inside. "Do you need help in the kitchen getting things ready?"

"No, I'm fine. The coffee's easy. All I have to do is flip a few switches. As for the biscuits and such, I'll just make a double batch." She frowned, and then she added, "It will be a job making all of the eggs, bacon, and sausage for the biscuits, though. Do you think Greg would mind if I called him in early?"

My mother had neatly sidestepped my offer to help her in the kitchen, but I didn't mind. I knew that I couldn't hold a candle to her, or my husband, when it came to preparing diner food. "He'd be offended if you didn't. I'd be happy to call him for you, if you'd like."

She pointed behind me to the folks already lining up to get into The Charming Moose. "I'm happy to do it. Besides, you're going to have your hands full out here soon enough. It seems that this fire has woken up everyone in town."

"Then we'd better get busy," I said as Ellen tapped on the door with her keys. She was our early morning to mid-afternoon waitress, and we couldn't run the place without her.

"I heard about the fire," she said as I let her in. "Everybody in town must be awake."

"Come on in," I said.

Before I could close the door behind her, though, Hank Brewer called out from the crowd, "How about us, Victoria?"

"Five more minutes, folks," I said.

"Four would be better," Reverend Mercer said as he rubbed his hands together.

"Four it is, then," I said with a smile as I locked the door again.

"We're going to be crazy busy in a few minutes," Ellen said.

"Don't worry. Mom can handle it, especially with Greg helping."

"Your husband's here?" she asked as she hung her jacket up on the peg near the door to the kitchen.

"Not yet, but I've got a hunch that he will be. In about half an hour, I'm going to deliver a care package to the firefighters. Will you be able to handle everything here when I leave?"

"You know I will," Ellen said with a smile. "Did you happen to see Wayne while you were there?" Wayne was her boyfriend, as well as being an automobile mechanic and a volunteer firefighter.

"As a matter of fact, I did. He was working the hose with the rest of his crew. He looked pretty manly doing it, if you ask me."

Ellen smiled. "Are you sure I shouldn't make that delivery myself?"

I understood her motivation, but I was hoping to get more out of the fire chief when I dropped off the coffee and food. "Sorry, but I've got some other business I have to look into while I'm there. Maybe next time, though."

"Next time it is," Ellen said as she started setting up the tables. "We've got two minutes left," she called out with a grin. Since she and Wayne had found each other, she was a great deal happier all of the time. I was glad, because she deserved someone good in her life. It didn't hurt that her kids absolutely adored him, and he clearly felt the same way about them. I didn't think it would be long before we heard wedding bells.

"One minute left," I said as I hurried into the kitchen. Mom was making biscuit dough at a quick pace as I asked, "Did you get hold of Greg?"

"He's on his way," she said, and then Mom frowned as she added, "and so is your grandfather."

"You talked to Moose?" I asked.

"He phoned a minute ago," Mom said.

"I wonder why he didn't call me?"

"He tried, but he said that you must have had your phone turned off," Mom said with a smile. "Don't worry, you're the only detective he wants to work with in this family."

I laughed. "I don't know. Martha might give me a run for my money."

Mom laughed. "Your grandmother is good at keeping your grandfather in line, but everyone knows that you and Moose are the true sleuths in the family. You two are going to dig into this fire, aren't you?"

"Why do you say that?"

"Victoria, you couldn't fool me when you were in first grade, and you certainly can't fool me now. I know that Barry Jackson threatened to take the diner away from us. You and Moose aren't about to sit by and watch that happen, are you? I just hope you both have solid alibis for the time of the fire."

"Do you honestly think that either one of us could have done it?" I asked her, surprised by her comment.

"Of course not," Mom said quickly. "I just know how Sheriff Croft thinks. He'll take the facts that you three fought yesterday and the bakery catching fire this morning, and he'll jump to more conclusions than any of us will like. You have to nip this in the bud while you still can, Victoria."

"I hear what you're saying, but Moose and I have only found killers in the past. We wouldn't know the first thing about going after an arsonist."

"Well then, you'd better figure it out," she said, "because like it or not, you're both in this up to your eyebrows."

"On that cheery note, I think I'll go out front and help Ellen. Is the coffee ready?"

"I flipped all of our urns on as I came in, so we should be good in that department," Mom said. "Stall everyone for five minutes so I can get prepped back here, and then I'll take on all orders, at least until Greg shows up."

"Did somebody call my name?" my husband asked as he walked into the kitchen.

"You're a sight for sore eyes," my mother said as she kissed my sleepy husband's cheek. "Sorry to rouse you like that."

"Always glad to lend a hand," he said. "Especially when it's a worthy cause. Where do you want me to start, Boss?"

"Why don't you take over the biscuits and fixings, and I'll handle everything else," Mom suggested.

"I'd be delighted," Greg said as he walked toward his apron, but not before stopping and giving me a solid kiss. He grinned at me after, and said, "Good morning, Sunshine. I don't usually get to see you this time of day, do I?"

"I'm around this time of day all of the time if you'd like to hang out," I said as I smiled right back at him. "You could always sacrifice a little sleep and spend some time with me every morning if you'd like to."

He laughed out loud at that, a sound that was infectious in

its pure joy. "It's tempting, but then I'd rob myself of seeing you anew every day at eleven. We need to keep a *little* eager anticipation in our lives, don't we?"

"Smooth, Greg, smooth," I said with a laugh of my own.

"I hate to break things up back here," Ellen said as she popped her head back into the kitchen, "but the natives are getting restless out there."

"The coffee should be done by now, and we've got an all-star crew working in the kitchen," I said. "Let's get busy, shall we?"

As we both returned to the front, the crowd wasn't clamoring anymore, and in a second, I saw why. Moose was already there, a coffee pot in each hand as he poured enough to fill every cup in the place. He had on his old apron, and I had to wonder if he'd brought it with him from home. I prepped both urns for fresh batches of coffee as I smiled at Moose. "Glad you could come by and lend a hand this morning."

"Happy to do it," Moose said as he winked at me. "Besides, I haven't slept more than six hours in one night for thirty years. This gives me something to do."

"Well, we're happy to have you," I said. "Right, Ellen?"

She smiled. "With you two here working the front, I might as well go on home." We both shouted NO at the same time, and Ellen laughed. "Okay, okay. I'll stay."

As the three of us worked on taking our customers' orders, I was lost in the work until Greg came out of the kitchen wearing his jacket and carrying two large aluminum pans covered in foil. "Victoria, are you ready to make this delivery?"

"Give me one second to wrap things up here," I said. "Are you coming with me?"

"I thought I might," he said.

Moose stepped in at that moment. "Greg, do you mind if I do it? There are some things that Victoria and I need to discuss on the way."

Bless his heart, my husband looked disappointed for just a

second before he smiled broadly. As he put the food down on an empty table, he said, "That's fine with me, Moose. If you go with Victoria, that means that I can go back home and go to bed."

"For at least a few hours, anyway," I said as I glanced at the clock. It was just past seven, and my husband wasn't due back to work his regular shift until eleven.

"Hey, I'll take whatever I can get," he said as he kissed my cheek and left.

"We're not going to have enough coffee," I said as I looked at the nearly empty pots up front.

"Don't forget the extra coffee for the firefighters," Mom said as she pushed a large urn on a rolling table up front. "I cranked up the old equipment in back to cover what you'll need."

"That's great," I said.

"Are you going with her?" my mother asked her father-in-law.

"I thought I might," he replied.

"Look out for her, Moose," she said simply.

"I always do."

"And you look out for him," Mom said to me.

"It's a dirty job, but I suppose somebody has to do it."

Moose grinned at me instead of taking offense. "You bet your socks it is. Come on, granddaughter, let's get this all delivered before it gets cold."

I turned to Ellen as I grabbed my coat. "Are you going to be all right here on your own?"

"I'll be fine. I'd tell you to give Wayne a kiss for me, but he might like the attention too much."

"How about if I do it?" Moose asked with a laugh.

"I know for a fact that he wouldn't like that," Ellen said, returning his laugh with one of her own.

"Then we'll both be better off if I skip it," Moose said as he grabbed the urn. Sometimes I forgot just how strong my grandfather really was; I knew that I couldn't have lifted it. That urn gave me trouble when it was empty, and now it was filled to the brim with coffee. I grabbed the food instead, and Ellen held the door open for us as we left. Once we had everything situated in the back of Moose's truck, he drove to the burned-out bakery in the beginning light of dawn.

Chapter 3

"Is it possible that Barry could have burned down the bakery himself?" Moose asked me as he drove.

"Why would he do that? Last night, he told us that he was expanding the business and that he even had a backer to finance his plans."

"Victoria, think about it for one second. It would be the perfect insurance dodge, wouldn't it?" Moose asked me. "What better way to allay any suspicion that he torched the place himself than to come to the diner last night and pick a fight with me. He had no evidence that I tore down a single flyer of his, and yet he marched in there and shouted my guilt to anyone who would listen. It was a pretty spectacular way to get noticed in a crowded diner, don't you think?"

I started to dismiss the idea out of hand, but then I began to consider it in earnest. I had wondered about Barry's display of anger and why it had been directed at us. Moose's explanation made sense if I looked at it from his point of view.

"Well, what do you think?" Moose asked me as we neared the cordoned-off area.

"To be honest with you, I'm a little troubled by the fact that you're making so much sense," I said.

Moose frowned at my statement. "What's that supposed to mean, granddaughter?"

"Maybe we're both getting just a little too paranoid for our own good. Is it possible that we've been investigating murder for so long that we're actually looking for evidence of trouble without having any basis in fact for our suspicions?"

"I suppose it's possible," my grandfather said a little grudgingly, "but you're right more times than you're wrong when you take away the benefit of the doubt with most folks."

"Cynical much, Moose?" I asked.

"I'm just being realistic," my grandfather said. "Tell you what. I'm going to run my theory past the sheriff."

"We both know that he's going to think that we're just trying to downplay Barry's slip at the diner last night."

Moose pulled off to the side of the road when he got as far as he could before the barriers and shut off the engine. Before he got out, he turned to me and said, "Victoria, we both know that fall last night was staged. Neither one of us pushed the man down."

"I realize that, Moose. I'm just saying that's how it's going to look to some folks who weren't there."

"Well, I'm not too worried about that. Barry isn't going to get away with the fire or the extortion attempt. I'll see him dead first."

"Moose, you shouldn't keep saying that. Somebody might actually believe you."

He laughed, but there was a hollow ring to it. "Nobody who knows me would take that kind of talk seriously. I'm just frustrated by the whole mess, and I'm blowing off a little steam. There's no harm in it."

"That's where you're wrong," I said as I got out of the truck.

"What do you mean?" Moose asked as he grabbed the urn of coffee and the extra paper cups.

As I got the food, I said, "I know that you don't mean it, but it's something entirely different if someone else overhears you say something like that. You need to tone down your words a little."

He put the urn back down on the tailgate and looked hard at me. "Victoria, I'm not about to change my ways at my age. I've gotten through my entire life speaking what's on my mind, and I'm not going to stop doing it now. If other people have a problem with it, then that's just too bad, isn't it?"

"It might be," I said. "Do what you want, Moose. I'm just saying, it might make sense to calm down a little until we find out if Barry's really going to sue us or not."

"I guess I can see what you're saying," he said grudgingly as he picked up the urn again. "Maybe I'll do as you suggest."

What? Had I actually won an argument with my grandfather? If I had, it was a red-letter day. Moose might not always be right, but he was rarely unsure of himself. Maybe he was a little more worried about this mess than I'd realized.

"How much food did Greg make?" I asked as I struggled with the aluminum serving trays. "There's enough here to feed an army."

"Those volunteers have been working hard putting out a big fire," Moose said. "They're going to be hungry."

"You don't have a problem with me squandering our profits on this, do you?"

My grandfather shook his head. "Victoria, I've never been one to turn away a good cause. As far as I'm concerned, this is a part of what The Charming Moose is all about. Sure, I've always liked to see a profit as much as the next guy, but if we can't do something good for someone just because we can, then I don't want to be any part of it. Do you know what I mean?"

"I do, and I agree with you one thousand percent," I said.

Chief Yates spotted us, and he walked over in our direction. "Wow, you didn't have to do all this," he said as he relieved me of my burden.

"Happy to do it, Luke," Moose said. "How's it going?"

"It's mostly out now. We're hitting any hot spots we find, but truth be told, it's over." He looked down at the trays he was carrying. "This is all going to be greatly appreciated. Thank you both."

"You're most welcome," I said as I spotted a man walking alone among the ruins of the bakery. What had once been a fine old wooden building was now reduced to black charred rubble. The man standing directly in the center of the soggy mess wore a hard hat and sported a clipboard, and I noticed him bending down checking something out. "Who's that?"

"Fire inspector from the county," the chief said. "We were told to stand by, so that's what we're doing. Let's get our people fed." We all walked over to the men and women from the volunteer departments, and it didn't take them long to scoop up the coffee and biscuits.

Wayne, his face smudged a little from the fire, said, "If you see Ellen, tell her I'm okay. She worries about me." He added the last bit with a sheepish grin.

"I will. She wanted to come herself, but I needed her back at the diner," I explained.

"Understood," he said as one of his fellow volunteers called him over.

I overheard Moose starting to talk to the fire chief, and I listened to what they were saying.

"I can't say, Moose," the chief said. "I'm no expert. That's why we have him out there," he added as he gestured to the man inspecting what was left of the building.

"I'm not asking you to go on the record or anything," Moose said. "I just want to know what you think."

"And you won't tell anyone what I tell you?" the chief asked.

"Luke, you have my word," Moose said solemnly. That alone was good enough for anybody who knew my grandfather. His word was his bond, and he'd sooner rip off his own right arm than he would break a promise.

"It was intentional," the fire chief said softly. "There's no way this wasn't set by someone hoping to burn this place to the ground. That's my unofficial opinion, but I'd be stunned if the official one doesn't match it, and that's the truth. I've been doing this too long not to be able to spot such an amateur arson."

"Thanks," Moose said. "I appreciate that."

"Just remember, you didn't hear it from me," the chief replied.

Moose pretended to look puzzled. "Hear what?"

"Exactly," the chief said as he took a sip of his coffee. "Here we go. Now we hear the official version," he added as the inspector walked over to him in a hurry.

"Chief, I need you over here."

"What's up? Did you find the accelerant?" he asked.

"Something more than that," the man said. "Call the sheriff, would you?"

"So, it's arson after all," Chief Yates said smugly.

"More than that, I'm afraid. I just found a body."

The inspector looked shaken by the discovery, and the chief dropped his paper cup of coffee as he said, "You're kidding."

"Not about something like that. It looks as though we might have a homicide on our hands, as well as arson."

"I'll call Sheriff Croft right now," the fire chief said as he took out his cell phone.

"Is there any way to tell if it was Barry Jackson?" Moose asked the inspector.

The man looked surprised to find Moose and me standing there. "There's no way any identification will be made without dental records." He looked sick as he said it, and I had to wonder if this was his first body.

Chief Yates hung up. "He was at a hit-and-run on Mulberry, but he's on his way now."

"Good. Until he gets here, we need to secure the crime scene." The inspector was getting a little color back in his face, and it appeared that he was beginning to come to terms about what he'd found.

"Will do," Chief Yates said, and then he walked over to his crew.

The inspector turned to us and said, "I'm afraid you'll both have to back up a hundred yards. This is now an active crime scene."

"So, you don't think it could have been an accident?" Moose asked him.

"I'm afraid that's restricted information," the man said.

Moose and I faded into the background, and my grandfather tugged at my arm. "Let's go back to the diner,

Victoria."

"Don't you want to hang around and see what the sheriff finds out?"

"No, as a matter of fact, I don't want either one of us here when he shows up."

"Why on earth not?" I asked.

"Do you really want him putting us and the crime scene together in his mind?"

"No, not really," I said as we walked back to Moose's truck. "He's still going to know that we were here, though."

"How's that?"

"The coffee and biscuits didn't come from the bakery, and we're the only other place in town that serves them," I said.

"Then let him come to us, but why make it any easier on him?"

"You're right," I said as we got into the truck and headed back to The Charming Moose. "This isn't good for us if that really was Barry Jackson in there."

"I don't see it being in our favor no matter who it was," Moose said, "but you're right. If it is Barry, we need to find out who did it. Otherwise, we both might be going to jail."

"I'm all for avoiding that," I said. "But how do we go about doing that?"

"We do what we always do," Moose said. "We start digging and see what we turn up."

Chapter 4

"Where are we going?" I asked Moose as he turned in the opposite direction from the diner. "You realize that our diner is back there, right?"

"I built the place, Victoria. Of course I know where it is," Moose said. "We're going to Barry Jackson's house."

"Now?" I asked incredulously. "How's that going to look if we get caught there?"

"Not good," Moose said with a grin. "That's why we shouldn't get caught."

"I can see the logic behind your reasoning," I said. "But even if we do find something useful there, how's Sheriff Croft going to feel about us getting to it before he does?"

"We'll worry about that when we come to it," Moose said. "There's something I need to check out before anybody else gets the chance."

"You know something, don't you?" I asked my grandfather as he sped up. At the rate he was driving, we'd be at Barry's in less than three minutes.

"Maybe," he said with that grin that told me he was indeed hiding something from me.

"Come on. Tell me," I said.

"I might be wrong," Moose said. "Then again, we might uncover something that was better left unseen, if you know what I mean."

"I honestly don't have a clue what you mean," I said, getting a little frustrated by my grandfather's reticence to talk.

"Be patient, Victoria," he said.

"I'm going to remember that advice the next time that I know something that you don't," I said.

"I don't doubt it for one second. We're here," he said as he approached Barry's house.

"Shouldn't we stop, then?" I asked as we passed it.

"Not if we're going to circle around and go in the back

way," Moose said. "Barry's car is gone, so I'm guessing that he's not home."

"That's probably a safe assumption, considering what they found at the bakery," I said.

"We don't know for sure yet that it was Barry," Moose said.

"No, but it makes the most sense. Who else would be there that time of morning?"

"The arsonist, for one," Moose said as he pulled down the alley behind Barry's house.

"I thought you believed that was Barry," I said as he parked and we both got out.

"It's the strongest possibility, but that doesn't mean that it couldn't have been anyone else. Victoria, we need to proceed cautiously here."

"Don't we always?" I asked as we crept through the yard. Instead of going straight to the house, though, Moose detoured over to an outbuilding. It was eight feet by twelve, and the architecture of it matched the house perfectly, down to the forest-green siding and the cream-colored trim. "Why are we going over here first?"

"Because unless I'm mistaken, this is where all of the secrets are hidden," Moose said cryptically.

"What are you talking about?" I asked him as we neared the small building.

"I went fishing with a chatty contractor a few years ago," Moose said. "The man wouldn't shut up, and he kept scaring away all of the fish, so I never invited him back."

"Okay," I said. "I had a friend in high school who started to sing her sentences every time she got nervous."

Moose stopped and looked at me oddly. "What has that got to do with anything?"

"Not a thing. I just thought we were sharing irrelevant stories," I said.

"Victoria, there's more to my story, if you'd let me finish."

"Go on then," I said, "because that's all I have about

mine."

My grandfather shook his head, and then he continued. "One of the things this guy talked about was an outside office he built that matched the main house. It didn't take me long to figure out he was talking about Barry Jackson, since he kept using different references to baking."

"Okay, I suppose that's a little relevant," I admitted.

"Just wait. It gets better," Moose said as he stood on the four-by-eight-foot porch. "He told me about a few secrets he'd been told to build into the thing."

"If they were secrets, why did he tell you?" I asked.

"What can I say? He's a pretty decent contractor, but the man can't keep his mouth shut on a bet. Hang on a second. Yes, this must be it."

I looked where Moose was reaching, and all I saw was a small medallion over the door, a decorative flourish that gave the tiny building a nice architectural touch. To my surprise, Moose reached up and grabbed it, turning it ninety degrees to the right. As he did, something clicked in place, and the front door opened of its own accord.

"How did you do that?"

My grandfather just grinned at me. "That's just one of the secrets here."

"How many are there?" I asked as we stepped inside the small eight-by-eight-foot room. The place was sparse, with a simple uncluttered desk under one window and a swivel chair under the other. The walls were blank slates, and the back wall itself had nothing but a coat of paint on it.

"There's at least one more trick that I know of," Moose said as he got down on his hands and knees. Instead of the molding going all the way across the floor where the walls met in the corners, there were small blocks of wood on each edge the molding butted into. In the center of each block was a turned wooden button, and as my grandfather pressed the middle of the one on the left, I heard another click, and the entire flat piece of molding along the back wall swung open slightly.

"What is it with people and their secret panels?" I asked, recalling our time at the pickle palace not that long ago with a chauffeur who had ended up being so much more than that in the end.

"That's what clicked with me when we saw the burned-out bakery this morning," Moose said with a smile. At least this secret panel wasn't big enough to lead anywhere. It wasn't even deep enough for a small cat to crawl into. As I looked at it a little closer, I saw that it was really nothing more than a hidden shallow drawer, and as Moose pulled it out, I saw a collection of papers inside. Evidently this was where Barry had stored anything important to him, and I couldn't wait to go through the things that we'd just found there.

That's when I had my first inkling that maybe my grandfather and I should wait for law enforcement. "Moose, should we be going through these papers before the police get a chance to examine them first?"

"Why shouldn't we?" he asked. "Do you honestly think that Sheriff Croft would have ever found this on his own? If it weren't for us, this would have all probably been lost forever."

That managed to make me feel a little better. "I see what you're saying, but we still can't keep what we find from him."

"We won't," Moose assured me. "After we're finished here, we'll phone a tip into the station, or at the very least, we'll leave this panel open so that they'll find it themselves when they get around to checking this place out."

"I like the second option better than the first," I said. "One more thing, though. If there's something interesting, we snap a photo of it with my phone, but we don't take anything with us that might help the sheriff. Agreed?"

"Okay, I can live with that," Moose said.

"Then let's start digging," I said as I reached for the top layer of papers.

I started to spread things out on the desk as Moose went for the chair. After he sat down and wheeled it over to where

I was working, he grinned at me. "Hey, my knees are a lot older than yours are. I need to perch every now and then."

"I wasn't complaining," I said as I started looking at what we had. "Was there anything else in the secret drawer?"

"Just these papers and this," he said as he put a handheld microcassette player down on the table.

"What do you suppose that's about?" I asked. "I didn't even see it."

"It was buried under some papers. Let's play it, okay?"

"Fine by me," I said as I reached out and hit the Play button.

A woman's voice, small and tinny, came from the tiny speaker and said, "Barry, I know you're there, so stop screening your calls. It's Sandy. Again. Why haven't you called me back? You broke my heart, you know that, don't you?" At that point, the woman cried a little, but then she quickly got herself back under control. When she spoke again, there was a new resolution in her voice. "If you think you can throw me away for somebody else like yesterday's garbage, you're dead wrong. I'm not going to let you get away with it. You'll pay for what you've done to me. Don't even think about trying to run away from me, either. There's no place you can go where you're safe from me, and when I catch you, I'm going to—" Evidently the time on the answering machine cut off, because Sandy was interrupted by a dial tone.

"Wow, she sounded mad," Moose said.

"Mad? She was homicidal if you ask me. Which Sandy do you think it might have been?"

"It sounded like Sandy Hardesty to me," Moose said.

I looked at him in surprise. "How do you know Sandy Hardesty?"

"Just because I'm retired doesn't mean that I'm a hermit," he said. "I meet people all of the time."

"I'm sure you're just a regular social butterfly, Moose, but I really want to know."

"If you must know, she ran into me with her car in the

grocery store parking lot last month," Moose said. "I was in my old truck at the time, and you could barely see where she hit me, but we got to talking. I remember liking her. She had spunk."

"Maybe a little too much for her own good," I said. "I wish we could record that tape."

"Can't your magic phone do that for you?" Moose asked me with a grin.

"Not directly, at least not that I know of, but I do know something that might work." I dialed my home number, waiting for my own machine to kick in.

"Hello? Victoria, is that you?" my husband asked after two rings.

"Greg, what are you doing back home so soon?" Despite what he'd told us earlier, I wasn't sure that he'd go straight home.

"You and Moose were delivering the food, so I didn't waste any time heading back here to catch a quick nap before I had to go to work again. The thing is, I can't fall back asleep, despite my best efforts." He paused a moment before adding, "Hang on a second. If you thought I wasn't home yet, why are you calling me here?" he asked.

"I'm trying to do something else. Do me a favor and hang up," I told my husband.

Before I could explain my odd request to him, he promptly did as I'd requested.

I dialed the number again, and once more, my husband answered the phone. "Is this some kind of new game of tag that I don't know about?" he asked me.

"You never gave me a chance to explain my plan. I want to record something I found, but I don't have any way to do it but to call the house and leave it on our answering machine."

"Then it's not going to do you any good if I keep picking up, will it?" Greg asked good-naturedly.

"Sorry about that."

"I don't mind," he said. "Call away," and then, before he hung up again, he added, "I promise I'll ignore you completely this time."

I dialed my home number yet again, and this time it made it all the way to the answering machine. When I heard my own voice ask to wait until the beep, I hit the Play button again, and I managed to record the message in its entirety before my own machine cut me off.

After I disconnected the call, my phone rang in my hands. No surprise. It was Greg. "Did it work?"

"Like a charm," I said. "Thanks."

"You're welcome," he said. "Do you care to explain to me what that was all about?"

"How about a rain check?" I asked him.

"That's fine. Will I see you this afternoon?"

"I'm sure you will at some point, but I might not make it back to the diner by the time you get there."

"Take your time. I'll see you when I see you," he said, and then we got off the phone.

As I'd been chatting with my husband, Moose had been digging through some of the other papers. "Did you find anything else interesting while I was on the phone?" I asked him.

"More than you can imagine. This seemed to be Barry's favorite hiding place, because it looks like he kept all of his secrets here."

"Honestly, it's not that bad a place to stash things you don't want anyone else to find," I said. "What are the odds anyone else would have uncovered this stuff if he hadn't had a talkative contractor?"

"Not good," Moose said as he laid a note scrawled on lined paper on the desktop in front of me. "Victoria, check this out."

It was from Cliff Pearson, a man that I'd heard was on the dark side of the law, and after reading the terse note, there was not much doubt about who Barry's mysterious backer might have been for the bakery. Evidently, expanding the bakery hadn't been the only thing Barry had borrowed money for. The note said,

I won't tell you again. The next time you're late with a payment, you're going to get a reminder from me that you're not going to like. This is your last warning. From now on, pay me on time, pay the full amount you owe me, or I'll take it out of something besides your bank account. I'm not messing around here, Barry."

"Well now, that's not very friendly, is it?" Moose asked me with a grin.

"I wonder how much Barry owed him?"

"I don't know, but it appears that Cliff was pretty eager to get it back."

"At least the interest, anyway," I said.

"It sounds as though Barry wasn't going to be able to pay it," Moose said. "I've got to admit that if Cliff burned down the bakery, it was exactly the wrong thing to do if he expected Barry to ever be able to pay him back."

"Maybe he was sending a message to the other folks who owed him money," I said.

"That might work," Moose said. "Take a photo of it, and let's move on."

I did as my grandfather suggested, and then I put the note off to one side.

"What's this?" I asked as I picked up a stack of greeting cards bound together with a pair of rubber bands. After I removed them, I opened the first four pretty mushy cards, and a fifth that was anything but. Inside the last one, written in angry red letters, it said, *"Stop playing games with my heart, or yours is going to feel real pain."*

I showed it to Moose, who dropped it on the desk as though it had been on fire. "Where did he get these? That last message is pretty chilling."

I looked through the stack, and I saw the name Susan written inside the rest of them. "That's got to be Susan Proctor," I said.

"How could you possibly know that?"

"The swoop of that S is unmistakable," I said as I pointed it out to my grandfather. "She pays for lunch at the diner once a week with her credit card, so I've come to recognize that signature."

"Good enough. Take a shot of the signature on one of these cards," Moose suggested.

"Let's do one of the good ones, and the angry one, too," I said as I took the pictures. The battery on my phone was getting weak, a problem that I'd been having lately. "I don't know how many more shots I'm going to be able to take with this."

"Then let's make them count," Moose said. He picked up four torn fragments of paper and pieced them back together on the desktop. "Victoria, you need to get this one."

"What is it?" I asked as I studied the reassembled sheet.

"It appears that Rob Bester tried to buy Barry out at some point, but he clearly wasn't all that happy about the offer, or why else would he tear it up?"

"Do you think that's significant?" I asked Moose as I took the picture with my phone.

"I suppose that it could be," my grandfather said as he looked around.

"You know, Mom and I saw Rob at the fire this morning. He was standing outside the tire store with a garden hose watching the volunteer firemen."

Moose frowned. "It *could* be a coincidence. After all, if he's innocent, he'd want to try to protect his property."

"It gives him an excuse to smell like smoke, too," I said.

"We'll have to keep him in mind. Is there anything here that we've missed?"

I started looking through the papers again, and I almost missed the final clue. There was a bank statement tucked in with a series of bills, and I didn't know how those might help us find out who had torched the bakery and possibly killed Barry Jackson in the process. The statement said that Barry was extended over his credit limit, but what was really interesting was what Barry himself had scrawled on it. *"Get the money Mike owes you. Just because he's your brother doesn't mean that he can bankrupt you."*

I took another photo as my cell phone died. "That's it, Moose. I don't have any more juice in my phone battery until I recharge it."

"It appears to be all that there is to see, anyway," he said. "Should I shove this all back into the drawer and leave the release sprung so it will be easy to find?"

I glanced outside and saw a squad car pulling up in front of the house. "No time for that! We have to get out of here now. Just leave it all on the desk!"

My grandfather looked at where I was pointing, and we both hurried out of the building and rushed toward where we'd parked his truck.

"That was too close for comfort," I said as we got in and drove away before anybody could catch us there.

"I know. It was great, wasn't it?" my grandfather asked me with a grin.

"Why do you look so happy, Moose?"

"Victoria, we've got more solid clues to work with from the start than we've ever had before. Doesn't that make you glad?"

"I shouldn't have to remind you that we don't even know if Barry was murdered or not. There might not even be a homicide case here to solve."

"You heard the fire inspector. Someone died in that fire, and if it wasn't Barry, then he's our number one suspect. Either the information we found helps us find his killer, or it gives us a chance to name him as the murderer. Either way, that stash was a good find."

"It was," I admitted. "First things first, though. We need to find out who was in that bakery when it burned to the ground."

"Leave that up to me," Moose said as he started driving back in the general direction of the diner.

"Where are we going now?" I asked, though I had a pretty clear idea of our destination.

He tapped the clock on the dash of his truck. "Your shift starts in three minutes," Moose said. "Where do you think?"

"I thought I'd let Ellen handle things for the rest of the morning," I said. "If I have to, I can always call Martha."

"You could, but maybe you'd better save all of that until we find out if we're hunting for a killer, or a main suspect. Until then, we should go about our normal business, and that means that you need to work your shifts at the diner, like always."

"And what exactly are you going to be doing in the meantime?" I asked my grandfather as he pulled into The Charming Moose's parking lot. I had a sneaking suspicion that Moose might plan on doing a little digging on his own without me, and that was unacceptable on several different levels.

"I'm going to discreetly ask around and see if I can get that body's ID," he said.

"And why can't I do that with you?" I asked.

"Because the man I'm going to tap for information isn't going to say a word in front of you," Moose said flatly. "I'm sorry, but that's just the way that it is."

"Okay then," I said as I opened the door and got out.

"What did you just say to me?" Moose asked me as he leaned toward the open window.

"I just agreed with you," I said as I started to go in.

"Victoria, don't be that way."

"What way?" I asked as sweetly as I could manage. "What can I say? When you're right, you're right."

He looked even more troubled by that reaction. "I don't like this, not one little bit. Whenever you're overly pliant, it *always* spells trouble for me."

I laughed as I walked into the diner, but I didn't say another word. I did happen to think that he was right this time, but it was a lot more fun making him wonder what I was up to than just coming right out and saying it. I suppose that I had said it, but in a way that the truth sounded completely unconvincing. It was one of my favorite ways to lie, not that I usually made a habit of it.

The smile from our last exchange faded quickly, though,

when I saw who was already in the diner, apparently waiting for me to get back.

Chapter 5

"Hi, Sheriff. Did you come by to thank me for the coffee and biscuits this morning? You really don't have to, you know. It was our pleasure."

"I heard that everyone appreciated that, but this is about something else. Where have you been this morning, Victoria?"

Had he or one of his staff spotted Moose and me fleeing from Barry's outbuilding? "I always take a break in the morning, and then I come back for my next shift." I pointed to the clock near the register as I added, "See? It's eleven o'clock, right on the dot." I hadn't exactly lied to him, but I wasn't about to admit what I'd been up to with my grandfather. If he had anything on me, he was going to have to come out and tell me. I wasn't about to trap myself if I could help it.

Evidently he was just fishing. "Understood. Do you have a second to talk to me, or do you need to get straight to work?"

"I've got time. Just let me tell Greg that I'm here."

"I'll be waiting outside," Sheriff Croft said.

I ducked my head in the kitchen and saw Greg and my mother chatting. "I'll be back in a second."

"To be honest with you, we didn't even know that you were here," Mom said with a smile.

"Then you won't miss me when I'm gone again," I answered and waved at them both. Greg winked at me, and I returned it as I left. I loved that my husband required minimal explanation from me for the oddest behavior, and it had really come in handy since Moose and I had started digging into murders together. Greg was there to support me, just as Moose's wife, Martha, was there for him. Neither one of them had a burning curiosity about our amateur investigations, but they each gave us all of the encouragement we ever needed.

It was good being part of a family that knew how to complement each other.

When I got outside, the sheriff was waiting for me, but to my surprise, Moose was with him, too. "Did you two start chatting without me?"

"No. I wanted to, but Moose insisted that we wait," the sheriff said.

That was a point for my grandfather, and I felt a little bad about the way I'd teased him earlier. "Thanks. I appreciate that."

"I don't have much time, so I'm going to have to make this brief," the sheriff said. "We just made a positive ID based on dental records. No real surprise; the body we found in the bakery was Barry Jackson. Normally I would have held on to that information a little longer, and I'd appreciate it if you two don't tell anyone until I'm ready to, but what you did this morning was nice, and I thought it deserved something in return."

"You know that's not why we did it," Moose said, though in truth it had been at least a little part of my motivation.

"I know that; that's why I'm here. I figured that you two would have to dig into this, so I thought I might give you a little head start."

"What makes you think we're going to investigate?" I asked as innocently as I could manage.

"Let's not kid ourselves here. In the eyes of a lot of folks, you two should be at the top of my suspect list. Barry threatened to sue you both and take away the diner the night before he dies in a fire at his diner. That's motive enough in most people's minds."

"What about yours?" Moose asked him warily.

"I'm still looking at all of my options, but I'm pretty sure that neither one of you had anything to do with it."

Somehow it was reassuring to hear that. "Thanks for having faith in us," I said.

Sheriff Croft just shrugged. "Just so you'll both know, I'll deny it if you tell anybody that I said it. I just think that you both deserve a fair shake on this one, and I know standing on the sidelines and waiting for me to solve this case isn't either one of your styles. Just don't do anything stupid, okay?"

"You know we can't make any promises like that," Moose said with a smile. I wasn't all that certain that it was an appropriate response, but apparently the sheriff didn't have any problem with it.

"Remember, if you find something that might be useful to my investigation, I expect to hear about it immediately," he said. It was the perfect opportunity for my grandfather and me to come clean, but we were saved from making that particular decision when he got a call on his radio. "Sorry, but I've really got to run now."

After he was gone, Moose looked at me intently. "You were about to tell him what we found, weren't you?"

"I was considering it," I admitted.

"Chances are that was what his call was about. He'll find out everything that we know soon enough. The one good thing is that at least we can stop guessing about who was in that building when it caught fire."

"We still don't know if it was intentional murder, though," I said.

"The fire chief clearly thought it was," Moose said.

"Should I ask Martha to take my shift so we can start digging around and try to find out?"

"At this point I guess that it's not a bad idea. Victoria, it won't do us any good thinking that what happened to Barry was just an accident," he said. "You know that my wife is always happy to help out at the diner, and this is important. We need to get to these folks before the police intimidate them all so much that they shut up and stop talking to anyone. If they don't realize they are suspects yet, we might just be able to get something useful out of them."

"That sounds like a plan. I'll call Martha, and you go tell Greg and Mom what we're up to," I said.

Moose started to go inside, but then he paused for a

second at the door. "I wasn't going to do anything without you. You know that, don't you?"

"I do," I said with the warmest smile I had. "Sorry I teased you a little before."

"No doubt I had it coming," my grandfather said with a laugh. "If not for that, then surely for something else. Make that call, I'll spread the word inside, and then we can get cracking."

It wasn't quite that simple, but Martha agreed to fill in for me. Fifteen minutes later, after Moose and I grabbed a bite to eat while we were waiting for my grandmother to show up, we were ready to start investigating based on the information that we'd just uncovered. We had a bit of a head start on the police, but there wasn't any time to squander. Still, we'd had to eat, and I knew that I sleuthed better on a full stomach than one that growled, and that went triple for my grandfather.

"To tell you the truth, I don't even know where to start," Moose said as we finally left the diner. "In all the cases we've investigated together up until now, we've never had so much information from the very beginning, Victoria. It's almost an embarrassment of riches."

"I know," I answered as we got into my grandfather's truck. "Who knew Barry Jackson would have ever inspired so many people to want to see him dead?"

"I have a feeling only one of them hated him that much," Moose said. "The question is, which one?"

"I don't know, but we'd better get started before the sheriff finds that stash."

"It won't be that hard, since we left everything out on the desk and the door to the office ajar," Moose said.

I looked at my grandfather. "Is that a hint of disapproval I hear in your voice?"

"We should have made it at least a little bit of a challenge for him," he said.

"That wasn't our deal," I said with a smile. "We did the

right thing, and you know it."

"I suppose so," he said. "So, which of our suspects should we tackle first?"

"I'd say we go talk to Cliff Pearson first," I said.

"Any reason in particular?"

"I believe that note threatening Barry's life is a pretty compelling reason," I said.

"I'm not so sure," Moose said, "but he's as good a place to start as any."

Moose did a U-turn and headed out toward Briar Falls. I looked at my grandfather and asked, "Do you know something that I don't?"

"From what I hear around town, Cliff can be found most days at Starlight Bowling," Moose said. "It's in Briar Falls, so if we're going to have a chat with him, that's where we should start looking."

"I'm not talking about that," I said. "I mean the fact that you're not so sure about him possibly being guilty of the murder."

"Think about it, Victoria. From the note we found, it's clear that Barry owed him money."

"So?"

"How's Cliff going to get it back now?" Moose asked.

"That's a fair question," I said. "Should we start with someone else, then?"

"We can probably talk ourselves out of every one of our suspects if we try hard enough," Moose said as he continued to drive. "Let's just speak with as many as we can find, and then see where we stand. Besides, the bowling alley isn't all that far away."

"You've convinced me," I said.

We discussed several ways of approaching Cliff on the drive to Briar Falls, but by the time we got to the bowling alley, my grandfather and I hadn't been able to come up with anything all that original.

"Let's just wing it, shall we?" Moose asked.

"Fine by me, as long as I'm following your lead," I

replied. My grandfather was good at extemporizing, and I always enjoyed watching him spin one of his webs, even when we were tracking down a killer.

The bowling alley was hopping with senior citizens when we got there, and I knew there had to be some kind of league play going on. They were all clustered at one end of the alleys, and I watched as two older men high-fived after one bowled a strike. It made me smile to see that they were both grinning like teenagers.

On the other end of the lanes, one man bowled alone. It was Cliff Pearson. I started toward him when Moose touched my shoulder lightly. "Hang on a second. He's almost finished," my grandfather said as he pointed to the overhead scoreboard. It was the last frame, and Cliff had already broken two hundred. I couldn't have done that the last time I'd bowled if I'd added up the scores of all three of my games.

We both watched as Cliff bowled again, collecting a strike himself as the pins all danced to the floor, but there was no joy or even acknowledgment on his face. It was as though he was required to throw so many balls a day, and the outcomes couldn't have been less important to him.

As he finished and started changing his shoes, Moose nodded to me and we approached him.

"Nice game," Moose said as Cliff saw us.

"Yeah. Not bad," Cliff said. "Are you here to bowl? You need to go to the desk over there."

"Actually, we're here to talk to you. Did you hear about what happened in Jasper Fork this morning?"

"No, but then again, I'm not big on the local news," Cliff said as he went back to tying his shoes.

"You might be interested in this. Someone burned the town's only bakery to the ground," my grandfather explained.

It may have been my imagination, but that information caused Cliff to pause for a moment before he finished his task. "That's too bad. I suppose you'll have to go somewhere else for your cupcakes now."

"Don't pretend that you don't know who we're talking about," Moose said, the nice tones now gone from his voice. "We know for a fact that you're out a lot more than access to baked goods. You're never getting your money back from Barry Jackson now."

"What money are you talking about?" Cliff asked. His tone of voice now matched Moose's, and the two men were clearly done with their feigned pleasantries. "You need to be careful, old man."

Moose started to say something, and I was pretty sure that it would be inflammatory, so I decided that it was time for me to chime in. "We just want to know how you expect to recoup your investment now."

"I don't know what you're talking about," Cliff snapped as he shot a finger at the man behind the counter. I hadn't noticed him before, but I did as he walked toward us. He was a big guy, a real bruiser, and the black eye he sported told me that he wasn't a stranger to physical confrontation.

"It's an easy question," I said.

"That I'm not going to answer," Cliff said as the hulk approached us.

"I just figured it out," Moose said as he turned to Cliff. "It was a message, wasn't it?"

"What are you talking about?" The thug got closer, but Cliff held up one hand, and the man stopped where he stood.

"You wanted everyone else who owed you money to know that you weren't messing around. How long will it take for word to get around that if your other clients don't pay up promptly, they might have little fires of their own soon?"

Cliff smiled at that, something that actually bothered me more than his threatening voice earlier. "That's not bad, actually. There might just be a way to make this pay off in the long run after all."

"So then, you admit that Barry owed you money?" Moose asked.

"I admit nothing," Cliff said. "All I'm saying is that hypothetically, the situation might not be a total loss."

"Where were you this morning around five AM?" I asked him.

"Are you actually asking me for my alibi?" he asked incredulously.

"I am," I said simply.

Cliff shook his head. "It shouldn't come as a big surprise to you that I'm not going to answer that either, but just to show you what a nice guy I am, because you've been so helpful, I'm going to let you both walk out of here right now of your own free will."

"And if we choose not to?" Moose asked.

"Then Curtis and three of his friends will be delighted to show you the way," Cliff said as three other men appeared from the office behind the desk.

"Thanks for the offer, but we know the way out on our own," I said as I took Moose's arm.

My grandfather was reluctant to go with me, but I finally managed to persuade him that it was time to leave.

Once we were back outside, Moose pulled his arm free. "We didn't have to leave, Victoria."

"Are you kidding? I didn't want to ruin the Senior Bowling League," I said. "Just think about what a mess you would have made handling all those thugs on your own."

"I could have stood my ground with them," Moose said, though he knew just as much as I did that it was a ridiculous premise.

"I'm sure that you could have, but this way you'll be rested enough to tackle the rest of our suspects."

"Who did you have in mind next?" he asked me as he started the truck engine.

"I'd like to have a chat with Sandy myself. The last I heard, she was working at the Starlight Diner out on Route 70 near Laurel Landing."

"Fine," Moose said. "We can even order some pie while we're there."

"You're not really still hungry after all we had for lunch, are you?" I asked. My grandfather could put it away, but I was still a little surprised that he could eat anything so soon after lunch.

"Pie doesn't count, Victoria," Moose said. "There's always room for that."

"Fine by me," I said. "I'm just having sweet tea myself."

"You say that now, but wait until you see their display case. I'm guessing that you won't be able to refuse."

I was indeed a fan of the diner's desserts, as my waistline attested whenever I went there. "Maybe we could just split a piece."

He laughed heartily at my suggestion. "Dream on. If you want some pie, you'd better order it yourself, because I'm not about to share."

"I know that all too well," I said. Now that my grandfather was in a little better mood, I asked him, "What do you think about Cliff Pearson's reaction to the news about Barry Jackson?"

Moose hesitated a moment, and then he said, "My first impression was that he didn't know about the fire until we told him. Did you see him pause when he heard the news?"

"Maybe he was trying to think of something to say," I said.

"Exactly. If he'd been responsible for it himself, he's the kind of guy to have a story ready for the cops or anyone else who asked him about it."

"So, you think he's innocent?" I asked.

Moose laughed at the suggestion. "Victoria, I doubt that man came out of the womb innocent, but my gut tells me that he didn't kill Barry Jackson. The money Barry owed him had to mean more to him than a lesson in the pitfalls of not paying to his other customers. Cliff looked genuinely pleased when I suggested that it might be a warning, so I doubt that was his motive. Word is going to get out that Barry wouldn't or couldn't pay and that Cliff took steps to punish him, but I doubt that the rumors will be any truer than most of the other gossip we hear."

"I see your point," I said, "but I'm not ready to strike his name off our list permanently just yet."

"We can leave him there as far as I'm concerned too, but in the meantime, I think we should focus on the other suspects on our list. I hope we don't add too many more names to it in the course of our investigation. We're already drowning in the possibilities."

"Who knew that a baker could make that many people angry enough to kill him?"

"I don't know, but we need to find out before folks start questioning our own involvement in the case," Moose said.

"You're right. This is one case we need to solve, and fast."

Chapter 6

"I don't see Sandy anywhere, do you?" I asked Moose as we walked into the Starlight Diner in Laurel Landing. The place looked as though it had been scooped up straight from the fifties and brought forward in time. The floor was tiled with alternating black and white linoleum squares, the booths were all covered in shiny red vinyl, and the countertop was stainless steel. A jukebox played in one corner, and the waitresses on duty wore outfits straight from long ago.

"Let's ask," Moose said as he approached one of the women waiting on tables.

"Have a seat anywhere you'd like and I'll be right with you," she said automatically as my grandfather and I approached her.

"We'd like to sit in Sandy Hardesty's section, if we could," Moose said.

She pointed with her pen as she said, "It's going to be over there by the window, but you're going to have to wait if she's the one you want. Sandy's not officially due to start work for another five minutes."

"Do you happen to know where she is right now?" I asked. "We'd love a chance to chat with her before she gets too busy."

She shrugged and pointed outside. "Sandy allows herself one cigarette a day before her shift, but she doesn't like to be disturbed when she's back there."

"Fine, then," Moose said. "Thanks for the information."

I hadn't really wanted pie initially, but my grandfather had gotten me in the mood for a slice. As he headed back for the door, I asked, "Does this mean that we're not getting pie after all?"

"Not right now," he said, "but maybe later."

We went outside and around the building, and there Sandy was, sitting at a worn-out old picnic table in back of the restaurant putting out a cigarette. "What are you two doing here? Don't you get enough diner food at your place?"

"We wanted to talk to you about Barry Jackson before your shift started," Moose said.

Sandy frowned, and then she stood. "What about him?"

"We understand you two had a bad breakup recently," I said.

"I wouldn't say that it was particularly bad," she replied, trying her best to feign an air of nonchalance that wasn't quite convincing. "It was more of a mutual agreement that we'd be better off seeing other people. Why are you asking me about Barry?" Her expression clouded up again. "Did he say something otherwise? Because if he did, the two of us are going to have ourselves a little chat."

"Relax, Sandy, we didn't find out about you from him. Well, at least not directly."

"What's that supposed to mean?" Sandy asked. "If he's been spreading rumors that our breakup was anything other than mutual, then he's lying, and I'll make sure he shuts his mouth from now on when it comes to me."

I suddenly realized that she must not have heard about the fire if she was telling us the truth. "Sandy, there's something that you need to know."

"Hang on a second," she said as she pulled out her phone. "I'm going to get to the bottom of this myself right here and now." I tried to tell her what had happened, but she held a hand up as she waited for an answer that wasn't ever going to come. After a few moments, Sandy put her phone back in her purse. "He's not picking up, the little coward."

"Sandy, he's not answering because Barry is dead," Moose said to her.

The waitress looked at my grandfather as though he'd just told her a bad joke in poor taste. "Sure he is. At least he's going to wish that he was after I get through with him."

"It's true," I said. "There was a fire at the bakery this morning, and they found him inside."

"No. No. I don't believe it," she said softly. "He can't

be."

"I'm sorry, but it's true," I said.

I watched a gamut of emotions run through her, and for a moment I thought she was going to lose it completely, but miraculously, Sandy finally sighed heavily as she said, "That's tough news to hear. The man wasn't all that nice to me in the end, but he didn't deserve to die." There were no tears or wails of grief from her. It was as though she'd already come to grips with what had happened. Or maybe it was just the end of her acting with us. If she'd set that fire herself, it was entirely possible that this was the way she'd decided to play it when Barry's body was discovered.

Either way, this woman was cold inside, icier than I could even imagine.

"Aren't you more upset than that?" Moose asked her. "You must have loved him at one point not all that long ago."

Sandy tried not to dwell on my grandfather's words. "I don't know if it was ever really love. What does that matter now anyway? He's gone, and there's no getting him back now."

"Sandy, we heard the message you left him on his answering machine," I said. We needed to crack through that tough façade of hers, and that was the only weapon we had left at our disposal.

"What message? I never left him a message," she said angrily.

Wow, she was actually going to try to deny it. "It's no use. We have a recording of it ourselves. Would you like me to play it back for you?"

I showed her my phone and started to dial my home number when she said, "Fine. So I left him a message a while back. I was upset, but I didn't mean it."

"It sounded to us on the tape like you did," Moose said. "Where were you this morning between five and six AM?"

"I was home, alone, in my bed and sound asleep. Where were you?"

"I was with my wife," Moose said, "but then again, I don't

need an alibi."

"That's not what I heard. Everybody's talking about it. Barry was going to take your diner away from you."

"It's not his diner," I said. "It's mine."

"Not for long, from the way I heard it. I suppose you were with your husband this morning."

"Actually, I was on my way to work for fifteen minutes of that," I said, realizing that I really didn't have an airtight alibi of my own.

"Victoria, she doesn't need to know that," Moose snapped.

"The whole world's going to know soon enough," I said. "Besides, I don't have anything to hide."

"Neither do I," Sandy said. "I didn't kill him, and I certainly didn't burn him to death. As a matter of fact, I'm afraid of fire."

"That's going to be hard to prove, don't you think?" Moose asked.

"Not really. When I was a little girl, I went camping with my folks. They were taking a nap, and I found my dad's lighter. I was playing with it, I dropped it, and the weeds around us caught on fire. I burned half of a national forest down before they could put it out. Ever since, an open flame scares me to death."

"And yet you light up a cigarette every day," I said.

"That I can't help. It's an addiction. You know who you should really be talking to?"

"Who's that?" I asked.

"Susan Proctor. She's the one Barry dumped me for. That chick is certifiably insane if you ask me. She could have easily gotten upset with Barry and lit him up."

"What makes you think she's crazy?" Moose asked.

"Have you seen where she lives? It's nothing but a hole in the ground. Literally." Sandy glanced at her watch, and then she said, "Listen, I'm sorry about Barry, but there's nothing else to say. I need to go now; I've got to go to work or they will dock my pay, as bad as it is."

We started to follow her into the diner when Moose's cell

phone rang. Sandy went ahead, and I started to follow her myself when Moose grabbed my arm. I stayed behind, and I heard him say, "Fine. We'll be there shortly."

"What was that all about?" I asked Moose.

"It was your husband."

"What's wrong with Greg?" I asked, worried that somehow this mess had come back on him already.

"Nothing. Someone is at the diner, and she wants to talk to us right now."

"Is it Susan Proctor?" I asked.

"No, though it would probably be better for me if it were. Holly is waiting for us there. She told Greg that she had something important to tell us."

"Martha must be pleased to have her there," I said sarcastically. Judge Holly Dixon was an old friend of my grandfather's, and though he swore nothing had ever happened between them, she was the one woman who could make my grandmother jealous. I had a hunch that she had a reason to feel that way, not that Moose would ever be unfaithful to Martha, but he hadn't been married to her his entire life, though he often claimed that it felt that way. All I knew was that there was some kind of history between the judge and my grandfather, and I wasn't really sure that I wanted to know anything more than that.

"We both know better than that," Moose said. The man was so distracted by the judge's appearance that he'd missed my sarcasm, a sure sign that her presence at our diner had thrown him off. "We need to get back to the diner right now."

"What about Sandy?" I asked.

"We can discuss her on the way, but I'm not sure what else there is to say. It doesn't matter right now, anyway; this can't wait."

"Fine. Let's go then."

It appeared that I'd have to have my pie later. I agreed with Moose, though. This had to be important, or else the judge wouldn't have come to The Charming Moose.

As my grandfather drove us back to Jasper Fork, I asked, "Do you believe Sandy's telling us the truth?"

"Which part of her story are you talking about?" he asked. "The part about the fire from her childhood sounds suspiciously convenient as an explanation for why she couldn't have done it."

"I might give it a little more credence if she hadn't been smoking when we got there."

"You don't buy her aversion to fire, do you?"

"Moose, a flame is a flame, and if something happened when she was a kid, surely it would have scarred her enough to keep her from ever having a lighter in her life again."

"Who knows? Maybe it's true. Then again, she could be a pyromaniac for all we know."

"She very well may be," I said. "I want to check out her story, and I'd also like to talk to Luke Yates about her."

"What do you want to ask Luke?" Moose asked.

"I want to see if there have been any other suspicious fires surrounding Sandy's life in the past," I said. "I have a hunch this might be part of a pattern."

"That's a good idea," Moose said, clearly distracted. He wasn't watching the road close enough as his front left tire drifted off the pavement into the gravel. "Sorry about that," he said as he overcorrected and got back on the road.

"Would you like me to drive?" I asked him.

"No, I'm fine," Moose said.

"Then pay closer attention, okay? I want to get there just as fast as you do, but I'd prefer to make it all in one piece."

"You're right. I'll be more careful."

I glanced over at the truck's speedometer and saw that he'd backed off a little on his previous pace. Moose was actually within ten miles of the posted speed limit, something I considered amazing given his agitated state, and his clear desire to get back to the diner as fast as humanly possible.

Miraculously, we got back to The Charming Moose safe and sound. My grandfather pulled up in front, a spot we almost always reserved for our customers, but it was clear that he was in no mood to wait a second longer than he had to.

Martha wasn't up front at her station when we got there, never a good sign.

Instead, Ellen was working the register.

"Where's Martha?" I asked.

Ellen glanced over at Judge Dixon, who was currently nursing a cup of coffee, as she said, "She's on break."

"Is she ever planning to come back?" I asked softly.

"Not as long as the judge is sitting over there," Ellen said. It was clear whose side our waitress was on in the war between my grandmother and the judge.

"Thanks for taking the register, then," I said as I hurried to catch up with Moose, who had already joined the judge at her table.

"What did I miss?" I asked as joined them.

"Holly was just about to tell me why she came by," Moose said as he kept glancing back toward the kitchen. He was in hot water, and what's more, he knew it, but there was nothing he could do about it at the moment.

"I'm sorry to just drop in, but I thought this was important," she said.

"And we appreciate it," Moose said. "What's going on?"

"I was at the police station taking care of some unrelated business when I happened to overhear the sheriff say something."

I stopped her. "Hang on, Judge. You're not about to violate any kind of ethics rule or anything, are you? There's no reason for you to get yourself into trouble on our account."

The judge reached over and patted my hand as her face softened. "Thank you for thinking of me, but this is fine. It's not privileged at all."

I hoped that Martha hadn't seen the familiar touch, as much as I appreciated the gesture. I liked Judge Dixon, but I loved my grandmother, and if I ever had to choose between the two women, there was no doubt in my mind that I was on Team Martha all the way.

"What did he say, Holly?" Moose asked.

The judge took a deep breath, and then she said, "The sheriff is threatening to bring in outside help if he can't wrap this case up in forty-eight hours. There's some hotshot state police inspector who is supposed to be really good. He's based in Raleigh, but I understand that he spends quite a bit of his free time over in April Springs."

"I've never known the sheriff to bring in reinforcements before," Moose said, clearly surprised by the news. "What's different about this murder that he needs outside help?"

"That's the thing. You two have caught more killers lately than he has, and I think he's worried you're going to run against him for sheriff in the next election, Moose."

"What? That's ridiculous," my grandfather said. "If he thought that, why didn't he say anything to me about it? We spoke not two hours ago."

"This just happened half an hour ago, so it's all brand new," the judge said. "Someone must have put a bug in his ear about you, and he's starting to wonder why you two are digging into murder again."

"The murder victim threatened to take our diner away from us last night not three feet from where we're sitting right now. Doesn't he think that gives us both reason enough to do something about catching whoever killed him?"

"Easy, Moose," she said in a calming voice. "I'm not accusing you of anything. I'm just telling you what's going on so you'll be aware of it."

"I appreciate that," Moose said. "Do you know who's behind this?"

"He's on the town council," she said with a nod. "Do I really have to say his name?"

"It's Kenny Starnes, isn't it?" Moose asked. "Don't bother confirming it. It all makes perfect sense. That man is a blight on this town, and I wish that he'd never been elected."

I knew that Kenny Starnes and my grandfather had been in one argument or another for the last thirty years, and I doubted either man could remember what their original disagreement had been about. All I knew was that they intensely disliked each other, and I prayed for the councilman's safety every day. If anything ever happened to him, Moose would be the first suspect on everyone's list, including the sheriff's.

"Anyway, I just thought you should know," the judge said, and then she stood. As we joined her, she asked me, "What do I owe you?"

"It's on the house," I said. "Thanks for stopping by."

"Thank you, Victoria." The judge turned to Moose, and she was clearly about to say something. At the last second she must have changed her mind, because she left without another word.

I knew why a second later when my grandmother came out of the kitchen.

Much to his credit, instead of trying to run away, my grandfather headed straight toward her. As they spoke, I wondered how this new development would impact our case. If the sheriff was going to bring in outside talent, we didn't have much time. I doubted that a state police inspector would grant us the latitude that the sheriff had in the past. In fact, I wondered if we'd get any more preferential treatment ever again.

I don't know what Moose said to Martha, but he came over to me a minute later.

"So how are things on the home front?" I asked him.

"We're getting there," he said.

"Are you ready to tackle Susan Proctor now?" I asked him. "I don't have to remind you that time is of the essence."

"I know it is, but there's something else we have to do first, something even more important than our investigation."

I was eager to hear what that might be. "What's that?" I asked him.

"We need to speak to the sheriff and clear this up before

things get any uglier than they are right now. Any objections to that plan?"

"Not a one," I said. "Let's go see if we can find Sheriff Croft and straighten this mess out."

Chapter 7

"Sheriff, we need to talk," Moose said after we'd walked into the police station. The sheriff was standing by the front door, and it was clear that he was on his way out.

"I don't have time to chat, Moose," the sheriff said as he tried to brush past us.

"Is it an emergency? Because if it's not, this is important. I wouldn't bother you otherwise." Moose hadn't budged, and I doubted that many men in the county would have had the daring to block our sheriff's way when he was intent on getting past.

The sheriff stared hard at Moose for a few seconds, and I didn't like the expression on his face at all. Finally, he said, "Outside. You can have one minute and one minute only, so you'd better make every second of it count."

We all walked outside together, and though I hadn't been invited to join this particular conversation, there was no way that I was going to miss it, either.

"The clock's ticking," the sheriff said once we were all outside.

"Edgar, I don't want your job."

Sheriff Croft looked hard at Moose again after my grandfather spoke. I knew that the sheriff wasn't all that used to being called by his first name, particularly when he was in uniform, and I was just as certain that my grandfather had done it on purpose to get his attention.

"That's not what I heard," the sheriff said. "Either way, it doesn't matter to me. Moose, you're free to do whatever you want to."

"Are you really going to listen to Kenny Starnes?" Moose

asked him. "We both know that the man has had it in for me for what feels like a hundred years."

The sheriff shrugged. "The thing is, everything he said made perfect sense. Why else would you and Victoria keep digging into the murders that happen around here? It's clear that you don't have any faith in my ability to solve them, so it's the next logical step for you to run for sheriff yourself."

"It might be if I ever had the slightest interest in holding down another job, any job. The last thing I want to do is to run for a political office. It would be bad enough campaigning, but what if the worst-case scenario happened and I actually won? Do you think for one second that I'd want any part of your job?"

"Then why do you keep investigating murders?" the sheriff asked.

"Sheriff, my granddaughter and I have to get involved. If we don't, folks around here are going to assume that one of us killed Barry Jackson. Who knows? Maybe they think that we did it together. I don't have a clue. All I do know is that Victoria and I stay away from any crime that doesn't directly involve one of us, or a member of our family. Everyone knows that Barry threatened to take away The Charming Moose the night before he died, and worse yet, I threatened him. One of the EMTs who overheard us has been happy to spread that little tidbit around town. My granddaughter and I just want to clear our names."

"Then why don't you let me handle the case?"

It was a fair point, but I knew why we dug in ourselves. I was about to explain when I thought better of it and kept my mouth shut.

After all, this was Moose's battle, not mine.

"Sheriff, people will tell us things that they'd never dare mention to you, and you know it," Moose said. "Besides, between my granddaughter and me, we've got ties to every part of this community, not just the law-abiding folks."

"Are you saying that you knowingly associate with riffraff?" the sheriff asked with the slightest hint of a smile on his face.

"You've been in our diner," Moose said amiably. "As long as our customers pay for their meals and don't make trouble, we don't turn *anyone* away. Over the years, that's gotten us connections in all sorts of places that you might not have access to yourself in your official capacity." Moose put a hand on the sheriff's shoulder as he added, "I swear to you, I'm not running, okay?"

The sheriff seemed to think about it for a full ten seconds before he spoke, and then finally, he nodded. "Okay. Thanks for clearing that up. Sorry if I jumped to the wrong conclusions."

"With Kenny whispering in your ear, how could you not? Are we still good?"

"We are," the sheriff said.

"Does that mean that you're not bringing in reinforcements from the state police?" Moose asked him.

"How did you hear about that?" he asked pointedly.

"Hey, it's a small town. Word gets around. So, was it just an idle threat?"

Sheriff Croft frowned. "No, it's still happening."

"Between the three of us, we can solve this case without any help from the outside," Moose said.

"Maybe so, but I need to show folks that I can act decisively, and that's what I'm going to do. If nobody's solved this case within forty-eight hours, I'm calling in the big guns. Now, if you two will excuse me, I've got to run." He started to leave, and then he stopped and looked at me for a second. "I didn't mean to ignore you. See you later, Victoria."

"Good-bye," I said.

He grinned. "The real reason I spoke to you was that I just wanted to be sure that you hadn't lost the power of speech. You never said a word during that entire conversation."

"Hey, I don't have to talk all of the time," I said in mock protest.

Both the sheriff and my grandfather laughed, and instead of snapping at both of them, I joined right in. After all, I couldn't blame the sheriff for being surprised by the fact that I had remained silent.

In all honesty, it had kind of surprised me myself.

After the sheriff drove off, my grandfather let out a loud breath of air. "That was a close call. If I hadn't convinced him of my true intentions, it could have made the rest of our investigation a whole lot tougher than it had to be."

"You know, all in all, it's really not that crazy an idea," I said.

"What's that?"

"You running for sheriff," I said.

Moose looked at me as though I'd lost my mind. "Victoria, I meant what I said. I don't have the slightest interest in that job."

"Why not? There aren't any requirements that you be a law enforcement officer to run for sheriff. You know tons of people, so name recognition wouldn't be a problem, and besides, you're a crack investigator. This county could do a whole lot worse than having you in the job."

"As much as I appreciate the sentiment, I enjoy being retired too much to ever go to work again."

"I'm just saying," I said.

"Think about it, Victoria. Even if I wanted the job, which I don't, how do you think your grandmother would feel about me running for it?"

I laughed. "Sorry, I didn't even think about that. I doubt that Martha would be too pleased with it."

"That's the understatement of the decade," Moose said. "Now, where were we before we were interrupted?"

"We were about to go talk to Susan Proctor," I said.

"Then let's go pay her a visit at home," Moose said as we headed back to his truck. "Truthfully, I wouldn't mind getting another look at that crazy house of hers."

"If she even lets us in," I said.

"Why wouldn't she?"

"Moose, she's probably in mourning. After all, she just lost her boyfriend."

"I'll be sensitive," Moose said as he started driving, and I didn't doubt for one second that he could. My grandfather showed a gruff exterior to the world most of the time, but for those who really knew him, he had a soft side that was startling in its contrast to his public persona.

"I know you will," I said.

We got to Susan's place twenty minutes later. Driving up to it, it was hard to believe that there was even a house there. The raised grass slope seen from the road gave no indication that there was a home under there, with the exception of a single vent pipe coming up out of the grass. Susan's house was a tad on the odd side, and that was saying something for Jasper Fork. As we walked around, the house itself came into view, buried under the grass berm as though it had grown into the ground instead of out of it. A full array of windows faced out onto the woods. Her builder had taken advantage of the sloped hillside to tuck the house into the ground. I would feel like a mole living there, but it must have suited her, because she'd had it built especially for her after her first divorce. We didn't have to knock on the door to find Susan, though.

She was out front, tending to a roaring fire going in a fifty-five gallon drum. There were branches burning inside, a few beefier logs, and a stack of paper on top.

"What are you burning?" Moose asked her as we approached.

"Just some old papers I don't need anymore," she said as she threw the last handful into the flames. I noticed that there was a gas can on its side sitting nearby.

"It looks like you gave your fire a little help," I said.

"What can I say? I've always loved a good blaze. I've been meaning to do this for weeks, so when I got back home this afternoon, I decided it was the perfect time to do it.

What brings you two out this way? I don't get a lot of visitors." Her face was smudged with ash, and as we spoke, she rubbed a gloved hand across her cheek, leaving another gray streak.

"Did you hear about Barry Jackson?" I asked.

She frowned. "What about him? What's that man been up to this time? Every time I leave that man alone, he seems to have a knack for getting himself into trouble."

"There was a fire, Susan," Moose said.

Susan looked at my grandfather as though he were an idiot. "And it will still be going until I get everything burned that I want to get rid of," she said as she pointed to the blaze. "What's that got to do with my boyfriend?"

"I don't mean here," Moose said. "I'm talking about at the bakery."

Susan frowned. "I imagine that could happen occasionally when you're dealing with ovens and high temperatures," she said, clearly troubled by the news. "I should call Barry and make sure that he's okay."

That was the second time it had happened that day. She reached for her cell phone, but I stopped her. "You're not going to be able to reach him. I'm afraid that he didn't make it."

Susan studied me with a puzzled expression on her face, and then she turned to Moose for confirmation. "Is it true?"

"I'm sorry, but it is," my grandfather said, and Susan Proctor collapsed where she stood.

Moose grabbed her and kept her from hitting the ground as her voice filled the air with loud cries and sobs. There was obviously no use trying to talk to her at that point. "Let's get you inside," Moose said as he half led and half carried her to the house. There was a sofa placed just inside to take full advantage of the broad windows, and my grandfather eased her down onto it. She'd have a tough time cleaning out the smoky smell from the couch where she touched it, but I knew that wasn't an issue at the moment.

"What happened to him?" she asked between sobs as she

looked at us in turn.

"We don't know the entire story yet," I said.

"But it was arson," Moose added, something I hadn't thought she'd needed to hear yet.

"Are you saying that someone killed him on purpose?" she wailed, and then she was off on another set of hysterics.

"Is there anybody we can call for you?" I asked her softly. The woman was falling apart before our very eyes.

"My...my...sister," Susan said shakily.

I knew Elizabeth, but I didn't know her phone number. "What's her number?"

Susan handed me her phone as she said, "Just hit 3 on the speed dial."

I did so, and Elizabeth came on the line. "Hey, it's Victoria Nelson. Your sister needs you."

"I'm almost there," Elizabeth said. "I just heard what happened. I was going to call her and tell her over the phone, but I didn't want her alone when she found out. Are you there with her now?"

"Yes, my grandfather and I came by," I said, conveniently neglecting to mention that we'd come there to interrogate her.

"Bless you. Give me two minutes and I'll be there."

After I hung up, I said, "She'll be here in two minutes."

"Victoria, can you stay with her until Elizabeth gets here?"

"Sure," I said, puzzled by my grandfather's request. "What are you going to do?"

"I have to see about that fire," he said.

"Just let it burn," Susan whimpered.

"Victoria, we can't take a chance of letting it burn out of control," Moose said as he tried to disengage from her grip.

Susan wasn't having it, though. "Moose, you can't leave me."

My grandfather looked unhappy about it, but he turned to me and said, "If I can't do it, you need to go put out that fire yourself."

It took me a second to realize that Moose wasn't just playing fire warden and that he wasn't worried about the fire itself. He was concerned that what might be evidence was burning up right in front of us!

"I'm on it," I said as I stood and headed for the door.

"Don't go, either. I need you both!" Susan shouted.

"You'll be fine," Moose said. "Go," he said to me, and he didn't have to tell me again.

There was a garden hose near the barrel, and I opened the nozzle as I pointed it toward the fire.

Nothing came out.

I ran back along the hose looking for the faucet, and when I found it, I turned it on and raced back to the fire.

It was too late, though. The wood in the barrel was still burning brightly, but the papers on top had been burned beyond any hope of recognition.

Whatever Susan had really been burning was now gone forever.

Once Elizabeth arrived, we were quickly ushered out of the house.

Moose looked hopefully at me as he asked, "Were you able to save anything?"

"The papers were all burned completely by the time I got the faucet turned on," I admitted.

"It wasn't already turned on?" he asked me. "Are you sure?"

"Of course I'm sure. Why is that important?"

"Victoria, you've had enough fires yourself to know that you always make sure you have a ready source of water handy in case things get out of control. She had the hose nearby, but it was anything but ready. What was she burning?"

"Maybe that's not what was so important about the fire after all," I said as I got a sudden idea.

"What do you mean?"

"Moose, what if her having that fire was just an excuse?"

"I don't follow you," my grandfather said.

"Hear me out. If she started the fire at the bakery earlier, she most likely would still smell of smoke, and trust me, it's a tough scent to get out of your hair. Susan might have purposely set this fire to cover any traces of the smell from the earlier fire."

Moose thought about it, and then he nodded. "That's good thinking, Victoria."

"So, where does that leave us?"

"It's still way too early to say," he said as he reached for his phone.

"Who are you calling?"

"After my conversation with Edgar Croft earlier, I'm letting him know what happened with Susan right away."

"Is that how it's going to go from here on out?" I asked my grandfather.

"Maybe it should be," Moose said. "Victoria, I have to tell him about this."

"Agreed," I said. "Does that mean that you're going to tell him about what we found hidden in Barry's outdoor office, too?"

My grandfather paused, and then he nodded. "You're right. I should have told him about that earlier. To be honest with you, I'm kind of surprised that he hasn't found it yet without our help."

Moose made the call, and after an awfully brief conversation, he hung up.

"What did he say about Susan?" I asked. "I noticed that you didn't tell him anything about the clues that we found earlier at Barry's."

"He's on his way, and he even thanked me for the tip, if you can believe that. You're right; I didn't say anything about Barry's shed. Maybe we can tell him together."

"Do you think we should hang around here and wait for him?" I asked.

"I'm not so sure that's a good idea." Moose looked down into the barrel, and then he added, "Who knows? Maybe his crack team will be able to find something in this mess. All I know for sure is that we won't be able to."

"So, what should we do now if we're not going to hang around?" I asked.

Moose sniffed the air, and then he smelled his shirt. "I'll tell you one thing. We've got to do something about the way we both smell."

I smelled my shirt as well, and the distinct aroma of the fire hit me. "You're right. We can't go around investigating an arson case when we both smell like smoke. Why don't you drop me off at my place so I can shower and change clothes, and then you can go home and do the same?"

He frowned as he nodded. "We probably need to, though we can't really spare the time."

"I don't think we have much choice," I said. "I know we're losing the element of surprise the longer we wait to talk to all of our suspects, but there's really nothing that we can do about that."

Moose shrugged. "I guess that it was bound to happen sooner or later. The sheriff's going to be tracking the rest of our suspects down before we can get to them, so we'll just have to do the best that we can."

"At least Rob Bester won't be hard to find," I told Moose after he picked me up at the house. It had felt good washing the smoke off me, even if most of it had just been in my imagination. At least that's what I'd thought until I'd stripped down and stepped into the shower. As I shampooed my hair, the smell of the fire was strong, and it took a few rinses to get most of it out. Some of it would take a few days to finally leave. Did that make Susan brilliant in disguising her part in the fire, or was it just a coincidence? I wasn't ready to name her a killer yet, but if it *had* been a cover-up, she'd done a brilliant job of it.

"If he's at work," Moose said.

"Why wouldn't he be?"

"Victoria, that fire was right beside his building. What are the chances that his customers could get in there even if they wanted new tires?"

"I would think they'd come back," I said. "Tire shopping usually isn't that urgent."

"On the contrary, I've rarely shopped for tires when I didn't absolutely have to have them."

"I wouldn't know. Greg takes care of our cars, from tires to windshield wiper fluid to everything else in between."

"That's kind of sexist, isn't it?" Moose asked with a grin.

"Seriously? You can't honestly be asking me that."

"Why not?"

"Moose, in case you've forgotten, I own the diner, and I run it every day. My husband works for me as a fry cook, and he has no problem with me being in charge. Besides, he enjoys keeping up with the cars, so why shouldn't I let him?"

"Take it easy. I didn't mean to step on any toes."

"You didn't," I told him with a grin. "Besides, we both know who really runs your family."

"Funny, I like to think of it as a democracy," Moose said.

"You might like to think of it that way, but we both know that it's a benevolent dictatorship, with your wife in charge when it comes to the things that really matter."

Moose smiled at me. "I never denied it for one second. Hey, he's open after all," Moose added as he swung into the tire shop's parking lot. The barricades on the street were all down, though the crime scene where the fire had occurred was clearly roped off with police tape.

As we walked in, we found Rob standing by the front door, and we actually got a bonus as well.

Rob was deep into an intent conversation with Mike Jackson, the late Barry Jackson's brother, and as far as we knew, his last living relative, and more importantly, his only heir.

Chapter 8

"We're so sorry for your loss," I told Mike Jackson as my grandfather and I approached the two men. The overwhelming smell of cologne washed over me as we neared, and I had to wonder which man was wearing enough fragrance to make my allergies kick in. Maybe it was both of them. No matter, I was afraid to get much closer than we already were for fear of breaking out in hives. Besides, I'd just cleaned myself up, and I didn't want to go around town smelling like men's cologne. Whatever they were discussing so intently ended abruptly.

"Moose, Victoria," Rob said. "What brings you by my shop? Are you finally going to break down and get new tires for that truck of yours?"

"If I did that, the tires would be worth more than the truck, and we can't have that." Moose turned to Mike and offered a hand. "Sorry about your brother."

"So am I," he said. Mike was a run-down, beat-up version of his older brother, and if you'd asked me the week before, I would have said that there was no way that he was younger than Barry. It showed that he'd had a hard life, that was for sure, and it most likely hadn't gotten any easier with his brother's recent death.

"It can't be easy losing someone you were so close to," I said. "When was the last time you saw him?"

"We shared a drink at the house after he got home from the hospital last night," Mike said as he looked at me oddly. "Don't worry. I won't be pursuing the lawsuit."

"To tell you the truth, that hadn't even crossed my mind," I said, which was true enough.

"You probably couldn't even if you wanted to, could you?" Moose asked. "After all, it was his word against ours, and now he's not around to testify."

"That worked out pretty well for you then, didn't it?"

Mike asked loudly enough for a few of the other customers to notice.

"Let's all take a deep breath here," I said. I loved my grandfather dearly, but sometimes I wished that he had a few thoughts that he didn't feel the need to express so openly. "Mike, it's important that you know that we didn't have anything to do with what happened to Barry." I looked over at the charred remains of the bakery, a sight that was obvious from our position at the tire shop. "What's going to happen to the space now?"

"Well, as a matter of fact—" Mike started to say when Rob interrupted him.

"Nothing's in stone yet, Mike, so we don't want to jinx it, do we?" The tire man didn't look all that pleased about the subject being brought up, though I still wasn't sure what he was talking about.

That's when I got it.

"You're buying the lot after all, aren't you?" I asked.

"What do you mean?" Rob asked me. "I don't know what you're talking about."

He may have tried to brush me off, but Mike wasn't about to allow it. "Let her explain," Mike said to Rob, and then he turned to me. "What are you talking about, Victoria?"

"Barry didn't tell you about it?" I asked.

"Tell me what?"

"Rob tried to buy the bakery last month so he could expand his tire business, but Barry turned him down cold."

Mike looked at the tire man with fresh suspicion in his gaze. "Is that true?"

"It's all one big coincidence," Rob said as he tried to backpedal as quickly as he could. "Your brother and I just had an informal conversation a few months ago, that's all there was to it."

"It was more than that," I said, recalling the offer sheet we'd found in Barry's office that he'd torn up. "You made him a written offer, and he tore it into tiny little pieces."

"How could you possibly know that?" Rob asked as he

stared openly at me.

"We found the paper, Rob," Moose said.

"This changes everything. I need to rethink things, Rob," Mike said as he abruptly started to leave.

"But we had an agreement," Rob said angrily.

"Yeah? Try to prove it. I haven't signed anything yet," Mike said as he walked away.

Rob wanted to go after him, but he still had to contend with my grandfather and me. "Thanks a lot, you two. What good is an empty lot going to do him? I was going to take it off his hands and expand my showroom, but now I'm not so sure that's going to happen because of your meddling."

"Sorry about that," Moose said, clearly not upset at all. "Where were you when the fire started?"

"I was sitting at home by the fireplace enjoying a cup of coffee. There must have been some kind of plug in the chimney, though, because I got a backdraft and it blew smoke all over my living room. Who knew that as that was happening to me, poor Barry was dealing with a fire of his own?"

It was a convenient time to have a fireplace emergency; that much was certain. "Was anyone there who can confirm that?" I asked him.

"Sadly, since Rita left me, I'm all alone these days," he said.

"But I saw you at the fire soon after it must have started," I said.

"Like I said, I found out the bakery was on fire, so I rushed right over here to see if I could help. Now, if you'll excuse me, I need to talk some sense into Mike."

"Why don't we all go together?" I asked. "Moose and I want to talk to him again ourselves."

Rob looked at us for a few moments, and he must have seen that we weren't going to back down. In frustration, he waved a hand in the air as he said, "Forget it. I'll catch up with him later."

"Then we'd better be going," Moose said.

As we were walking away, I asked Moose, "That was interesting, wasn't it?"

"I imagine Rob will pay a great deal less for an empty lot than he would have for the entire bakery," he said. "Could he have been that cold blooded just to expand his business, though?"

"Why not? If Barry wasn't cooperating, maybe he figured that his heir might."

"That's assuming that Mike gets everything now," Moose said.

"Who else could it go to? I doubt that Barry left it to any of his girlfriends."

"You never know," Moose said as he looked around. "By the way, where did Mike go?"

I pointed to the lot next door, now a leveled charred ruin. "He's right over there."

"I feel kind of bad pouncing on him like this when he's clearly in mourning," Moose said.

"If it makes you too squeamish, you could always wait in the truck," I told him.

"I don't feel *that* bad about it," Moose said. "Let's go have a talk with our last suspect and see what he has to say for himself."

"Mike, do you have a second?" I asked the man softly after he failed to see Moose and me approach. Despite what I'd said to my grandfather earlier, I wanted to handle this as delicately as possible. After all, if Mike hadn't had anything to do with his brother's murder, the last thing he needed was someone accusing him of being involved, especially just after it had happened.

"What do you want?" he asked, clearly distracted by the remnants of his brother's former business.

"I know it's not easy, but we need to know something," I said.

"Listen, can't you two leave me in peace? I just lost my brother. We had an argument last night, and I said some things that I regretted almost instantly. I was going to apologize to him today, but now I'll never get the chance. Can you even imagine how that makes me feel?"

I was about to comment when my grandfather did it for me. "Was the fight about the money you owed him?"

I looked at Moose and shook my head, but he just shrugged. He was right. I'd been about to back off completely, but we couldn't afford to do that, especially not given the sheriff's timeline for calling in outside help. I knew that a state police inspector wouldn't be nearly as forgiving of our investigation as Sheriff Croft was.

"What money are you talking about?" he asked. "I didn't owe my brother a dime."

"That's not what he thought," Moose said.

Mike pivoted around and stared hard at my grandfather. To his credit, he didn't even flinch as he faced Moose down. "That's a lie."

"Show him the picture, Victoria," Moose told me.

"What picture?" Mike asked.

I got out my phone and found the photo I'd taken of Barry's bank statement. It was tough to see what he'd written beside it, so I tapped my phone and enlarged the photo. "If you still can't read it, let me do it for you. It says, and I quote, 'Get the money Mike owes you. Just because he's your brother doesn't mean that he can bankrupt you.' That's his handwriting, isn't it?"

Mike stared at for a few seconds, and then he looked away. "So what? That doesn't prove anything."

"You're kidding yourself," Moose said. "That's motive enough for murder right there, not to mention the fact that you're most likely going to inherit everything your brother had." My grandfather was guessing, but it was a likely enough scenario.

Mike just laughed, though there was an empty ring to it. "Do you think it's a prize inheriting my brother's estate? The way things look right now, there are more debts than assets. All I'm going to get from this is one big headache."

"What about this property?" I asked him. "Isn't it a part of his estate? It's got to be worth a small fortune all by itself."

"In the end, that's the only thing that's going to save me," Mike said. "I hadn't realized it, but he put the deed in both our names when he bought the business. I had a small slice of the bakery and I didn't even know it. Thankfully, it's not part of the estate at all, since there's a survivorship clause. It was Barry's way of reaching out to me." As he said that last bit, Mike's face clouded a little, as though he'd instantly regretted sharing that particular tidbit of information with us.

"Do you expect us to believe that you didn't know about it beforehand?" Moose pressed. "If you didn't, how did you find out about it so quickly now? Your brother's just been dead for a few hours."

"His attorney came by to see me," Mike said. "He wanted me to know the score before I did anything stupid. Barry told him that he didn't want me to know that I owned a small part of his business. It was going to be a surprise once things really took off."

"So, he didn't want you to do anything stupid like selling the land to Rob Bester; is that what you're talking about?" I asked.

Mike looked at me sharply. "Something exactly like that. The man turned out to be some kind of ghoul, if you ask me. He came out the second I got here and started hammering away at me about selling off this useless land to him."

"It's not as useless as he might like you to believe," Moose said. "It's a prime location, and there's a clean slate here now, so it will be easy enough to start over with something new."

"Probably, but I'm not going to be the one to do it. I just want this nightmare over with."

"I can understand that," I said. Rob's actions didn't make him all that great of a human being, but it didn't make him a killer. That was still to be determined.

"We both get it," Moose added, "but we'd still like to

know about that money you borrowed from your brother."

I could see in Mike's gaze that Moose had finally pushed him just a little too hard that time. "I don't have to tell you anything."

He started to walk away as Moose said, "We might not be able to make you talk, but the police certainly can."

"Then I'll save my answers for them," he said.

Before he could get completely away, I called out, "Where were you this morning when the fire started?"

He didn't even look back at us as he got into a beat-up old Honda and drove away.

"I probably shouldn't have asked him for an alibi," I said.

"Don't blame yourself. I'm the one who ran him off."

"Why did you ask him about the money he owed Barry?" I asked my grandfather. "Do you think it's relevant?"

"It very well could be, but the real reason I asked was because I was curious. Aren't you?" Moose asked me.

"Maybe, but there were other things we needed to find out more urgently, and now we've lost the opportunity."

"Victoria, I'm sorry about that, but I have a hunch he wasn't exactly in a sharing mood after he told us about the land. Did you see his face after he let that slip? I'm positive that he didn't want us to know that."

"Well, it does supply him with more of a motive for murder, doesn't it?"

"As if owing his brother a small fortune and not having to pay it back wasn't enough before," Moose said.

"Maybe so," I said. "Have we spoken with all of our suspects?"

"The ones we have so far," Moose said.

"And where do we stand?"

My grandfather smiled as he admitted, "Right where we usually are at this stage of our investigations."

"And where exactly is that?"

"Dazed, Confused, Overwhelmed, and Clueless," he replied.

"That sounds about right," I said with a grin. "So, what do

we do now?"

"I say we go back to The Charming Moose and get a little work done there until something else turns up," my grandfather said.

"Does that mean that you're going to work at the diner today, too?" I asked him.

"Heck no. I'm collecting my wife and we're going home. Running a diner is for you young folks."

"Moose, you could run circles around most people half your age, and you know it."

He grinned at me. "Maybe so." It was clear that he loved being complimented on his energy level. "But honestly, I could still use a nap after the day we've had."

"I could myself," I said, "but I'm not leaving Martha up front any longer than I have to. She's been great stepping in and covering for me, but right now, you're exactly right; I belong at the diner."

"I felt the exact same way myself when I was running the place."

"I guess it goes with the territory," I said as we headed back to Moose's truck and got in. It was a short drive back to The Charming Moose, and honestly, I was looking forward to a little time working there to take my mind off murder. Things had a tendency of getting intense when Moose and I were investigating crime, and it was a nice break when I got a chance to return to my old routines. Besides, I might even be able to come up with our game plan for later if I got lucky. It worked that way sometimes. Actively forgetting about suspects, motives, and clues allowed my subconscious mind to chew on the case while I was involved doing something else. Hopefully this time it would work as well, but if nothing else, at least I'd get a taste of my normal life in the peace and quiet that came with running the diner, even if for a few brief moments.

For now, we'd let all of our suspects simmer a little and twist in the wind without any help from us.

If we could figure out a way to get them all rattled, maybe

the killer would slip up and make a mistake. It was worth a shot, anyway, even if it did put our lives at risk.

That was just the admission price to this particular game that my grandfather and I were playing, and we were going to pay it gladly if it gave us a shot at catching a murderer.

Chapter 9

"How's it going?" I asked my grandmother when we walked back into The Charming Moose a few minutes later. She was back at the job she'd done when Moose had started the diner at the very beginning, and I didn't know what I'd have done if she hadn't been available to step in every now and then when I needed her. She'd gotten a little rusty at cashiering over the years, but the more I called on her to help, the better she'd gotten.

"It's been smooth sailing," she said with a warm smile that faded slightly as she asked, "Have you and your grandfather had any luck?"

"These things take time," I answered, parroting the response Moose and I usually had this early in an investigation. "I thought it might be easier given the number of suspects we found from the start, but honestly, it hasn't done us that much good at all."

She patted my hand gently. "Don't worry. Between the two of you, you'll figure it out."

"I hope you're right," I said, "but in the meantime, why don't you go on home and get some rest? I have a feeling that I'll be calling on you again tomorrow, if you don't mind."

"I'd be delighted to help out in any way that I can," she said as she gave up her spot behind the register. "Victoria, are you *sure* you wouldn't like me to stay a little longer?"

"I'm positive," I said as I settled back into my station. "We've done all that we can for the moment."

Moose was listening in. "That's right, Martha. Besides, it's nearly four. Jenny will be here soon, and then there will be too many employees hanging around and not enough customers."

Martha said, "Jenny's already here."

Moose looked around. "I don't see her."

"That's because she's in back. Greg's making her something to eat, something I'm certain he'd be more than happy to do for us before we go."

"You know what? That's an outstanding idea," Moose said as he started for the kitchen.

Martha grinned at her husband. "Why, because you're hungry, or because a pretty young girl who pretends to flirt with you is already back there?"

"Who's pretending?" Jenny asked with a smile as she walked out of the kitchen holding a plate with fried chicken, mashed potatoes, and brussels sprouts with cheese.

"Don't give him any ideas, dear," Martha said, matching her grin for grin. "The old wolf doesn't need a single bit of encouragement as it is."

"I can handle him; there's no need to worry about that," Jenny answered.

Moose looked at them both as he said, "I'm standing right here. You both know that, right?"

"Come on," Martha said as she put her arm in Moose's. "Let's go get an early dinner."

"Hold on. I'm not finished being offended yet."

"You can do it just as easily in the kitchen, can't you?" she asked him.

"I suppose so," he said as he allowed his wife to pull him into the back.

"I like your grandfather," Jenny said as she approached me.

"It's okay to like him, as long as you don't like him," I said.

She just laughed. "I'm no competition for your grandmother, and she knows it."

"Martha does have some kind of spell over him, doesn't she?" I asked.

"I need to ask her what her secret is, just in case I ever find a man who's worth keeping," Jenny said. I could tell that she was more than a little serious, though she'd said it in a joking tone.

"I don't know if it will help, but I can tell you what she told me before I found Greg," I said. "Would you like to hear it?"

"Are you kidding? Spill."

"She told me to find someone who's worth loving, and then never hold back. You might get a few broken hearts along the way, but in the end, if you're lucky, you'll find the love of your life, and when you do, never take them for granted."

"I'm not sure that I can be so daring with my heart," she said.

"You'll have a tough time finding love until you do," I said.

"Is that what you did with Greg?" Jenny asked softly.

"I got lucky there," I admitted. "I didn't have to kiss many frogs before I found my particular prince."

"I wish that I could say the same," Jenny said as a few new customers walked in.

"Give it time," I said. "Would you like me to wait on them? You've got a few more minutes before your shift starts."

"No, I've got it. Thanks for the chat."

"Anytime, Jenny," I said.

There was a bit of an early rush between the late lunches and the early dinners, and after that, our full evening crowd started trickling in, so I didn't get much of a break until it was nearly seven, the hour we normally closed.

I rang up our last customer as Jenny started cleaning the tables, and Greg peeked out of the kitchen.

"That last few hours just flew by," he said. "I love it when we're busy, with one notable exception."

"What's that?" I asked as I started balancing out the register.

"I didn't get to spend as much time with you," he said with a grin.

"We'll make up for that tonight," I said as I counted the

till and checked it against the totals on the report. "I don't believe it."

"How far off was your grandmother today?" Greg asked me with a smile.

"That's just it. The report and the till totals are spot on."

"Hey, she's been getting enough practice lately," Greg said good-naturedly. "Maybe she's finally getting the hang of it again."

"Are you saying that Moose and I have been gone too much investigating lately?" I asked him as I filled out the deposit slip.

"Not at all. I know that what you two do when you're away from the diner is important. I just miss you sometimes. Is that a bad thing?"

"I'd be hurt if you didn't," I said as I grabbed him and kissed him. He hadn't been expecting it, but he didn't look all that unhappy that I had done it, either.

Jenny walked by us and smiled. "Following your own advice, Victoria?" she asked.

"How good could it be if I didn't?" I asked.

"Am I missing something?" Greg asked.

"Never mind. It's just a little girl talk," I said.

"Then forget I even asked," he said with a smile.

I nodded as I released him. "Jenny, we can finish closing up. Go on and have a good night."

"You, too," she said.

I locked the door behind her after she left, and Greg said, "I'm almost finished in the kitchen. Would you like something to eat before we go?"

"As much as I love your cooking, I'm just not all that hungry," I said. "Are you?"

"I can always eat, but I'm good for the moment," he said.

After we finished cleaning up, we left the diner, making one stop at the bank for our nightly deposit on the way home. Moose and I had planned to get together in the morning when I took my first break at eight. We'd use my regular three-hour break for our investigation, and if we needed more time,

Martha had volunteered to cover for me again at the register and waiting on tables if Ellen needed her. I usually used my breaks to unwind a little, but when Moose and I were digging into crime, it was the perfect opportunity to track down suspects and clues. Besides, I worked the early shift from six until eight, which gave me a start on the day at my real job running the diner.

"How are things going with your investigation?" Greg asked me as we neared out house. "Or is it too soon to say?"

"You know how it goes," I said as we pulled up into our drive. "We tread water right up until the moment that it all falls into place."

"I get it," he said. "I know it's a bit chilly, but would you like to sit out by the fire tonight and roast some marshmallows?"

"Normally I'd say yes," I told him as I got out of the car, "but I've had more than my fair share of fire today. Do you mind?"

"Heck no," he said. "I'd be just as happy to curl up on the couch and watch a movie, as long as it's with you."

"You've got yourself a date," I said as we walked inside.

"Then I'm a happy man," he said. "I'll tell you what. Why don't you pick the movie tonight?"

We usually took turns, and neither one of us ever forgot who was next in line. "It's your turn, though."

"What can I say? I'm feeling magnanimous. Besides, you've had a harder day than I have. Just take it easy on me, okay?"

"Don't worry. If I pick a chick flick, it will be one you like," I said.

"That's all I'm asking," Greg said. I made some popcorn and we put in a movie, something light and frothy that helped take my mind off murder. Many times I loved my movies like I did my books, preferring gentle escapes rather than dramatic reminders of how cruel the world could be. If I wanted realism, I'd watch the news. What I liked was something that took me out of my world into one where light, love, and laughter prevailed. Greg tended to enjoy action-adventure movies, and I watched them willingly enough with him, but I knew that on occasion he enjoyed my choices just as much. Life was hard enough without injecting a little joy and laughter into it now and then, and one thing was certain. I never felt weighted down after watching or reading something gentle that offered me a few smiles along the way, some tender moments, and a conclusion that satisfied the romantic in me.

By the time we finished our movie, I'd forgotten all about Barry Jackson's murder. There would be time enough to tackle that again tomorrow.

Tonight, I just wanted to relish what a wonderful life I had.

"Chief Yates, what brings you by so bright and early?" I asked the fire chief the next morning a little after six AM. "You're usually more of a dinner customer than a breakfast one."

"To be honest with you, I didn't sleep much last night," he said. "Let's start with coffee, and go from there."

"I'm sorry that you had a rough night," I said as I filled up a cup for him and slid it his way. "Anything in particular I can do to help? I know I'm not a bartender, but I can still listen to my customers' woes."

"It's the fire," the chief said after he took a sip of coffee.

"I'm sure it's got to be tough on you," I said sympathetically. "Every time it happens, it must take a little out of you."

"Honestly, I never minded the fires themselves in the past. They've just been something that had to be controlled and contained, you know? I always thought of what we did as noble, you know? Does that sound too corny this early in the morning?"

"It's not corny any time of day or night," I said. "What you do is noble."

"Maybe, but when we find a body, it takes all of that out

of the equation. There's nothing honorable about recovering bodies."

The poor man looked tortured by what he'd found. "I don't agree," I said.

"Why not?" Was that a glimmer of hope in his eyes?

"Just think about how haunting it would be to the victims' families if you never found their remains. They'd be troubled by the absence the rest of their lives. At least this way there's some kind of closure."

"That's true," he said. "I had a cousin who went missing, and it took seven years to declare him dead, even though just about everyone suspected that he went fishing in the ocean and never made it back to shore. His poor wife didn't just have his absence to deal with, either. Everything was up in the air legally as well. It would have been a blessing if we could have found him, that's for sure." He stared into his coffee for a few moments, and then the chief added, "Not that there was any danger that Barry's body wouldn't be discovered. He was found sitting at his desk, about as obvious a place as we could have looked for him."

"Do you think he was placed there on purpose?" I asked.

Chief Yates looked surprised by the question. "I hadn't really thought about it, but I suppose it could have played out that way. One thing's certain. Nobody was trying to hide the fact that Barry was dead."

I thought about what he'd just said for a second, and I realized just how true it was. Whoever had set the fire at the bakery had clearly wanted Barry Jackson's body found. Did that mean that the killer was someone who would directly inherit from the victim? If so, that would put Barry's brother, Mike, on the hot seat. But he wasn't the only one. If Rob Bester had killed Barry to get to his land, he'd need Barry found fast as well. Then again, if Cliff Pearson had killed Barry to send a message to his other clients, he'd need a quick discovery, too. That line of thought did reduce our list of suspects by two, though. There'd be no reason Sandy Hardesty or Susan Proctor would care if Barry were ever found or not if they'd set that fire. It was definitely an angle to pursue, and while I wasn't ready to write the ladies off quite yet, it did give me more reason to look into the men's motives, alibis, and opportunities.

As soon as Moose showed up, we were going after the three men on our list first.

Later that morning, I was about to catch my grandfather up on my new theory about the arson/murder when I stopped abruptly.

He looked at me with a puzzled expression. "Go on. Finish the thought, Victoria."

"Later," I said as I pointed over his shoulder.

Sheriff Croft walked through the diner door, and he didn't look happy.

"I need to talk to both of you right now," he said sternly.

"Would you like a cup of coffee first?" I asked as I poured some in a cup and started to hand it to him.

"Victoria, I'm not here for your coffee," he said. The sheriff glanced around the diner and spotted an empty booth that was a little isolated. "Over there should be fine."

"I'm not sure I like the tone of your invitation," Moose said. I put a hand on his arm and shook my head. This wasn't the time for either one of us to be truculent.

"We're happy to talk with you, though," I said quickly before the sheriff could react to Moose's comment. "Right, Moose?" I asked him pointedly.

"Right," he said. "Sorry. I had a rough night." There was a bit of hesitation in his voice as he said it, but I had the feeling that he'd understood the need to pull back some.

"You're not the only one. I understand, though," the sheriff said as the three of us took our places in the booth, my grandfather and me on one side and Sheriff Croft on the other.

"I've got to admit, that was cute what you two did," the sheriff said as he looked hard at both of us.

"What exactly are you referring to?" I asked him.

"Don't play coy with me, Victoria. I know that it was the two of you."

Moose started to say something, but I pinched his leg a little before he spoke to remind him that we needed to cooperate, at least for the moment. When he did speak, his tone of voice was mollified. "Sheriff, we really are baffled about the subject matter. What exactly was it that we were supposed to have done?"

"The secret drawer in Barry Jackson's office," he said. "Tell me that wasn't the two of you, poking and prying where you don't belong."

"I resent that," Moose said flatly.

"Resent it all you'd like. Just tell me that it isn't true."

"Sheriff," I said, "even if we did find this mysterious drawer you're talking about, why are you so upset about it? Would you have been able to find it on your own if someone hadn't left it open for you?"

He looked sharply at me. "I'll take it that is a confession, then."

"It's nothing of the sort," I replied, allowing a little snap in my voice as well. Sometimes I got a little defensive when I was accused of something, especially when the accusation was based on the truth.

He'd had enough of our verbal sparring. "I'm going to ask you both straight out right here and right now. Did you open that drawer?"

I was weighing the best way to answer when my dear sweet direct grandfather said simply, "We did."

"How did you even know about it being there?" the sheriff asked, clearly a little surprised by my grandfather's confession. "That wasn't something you could just stumble across without having a clue that it was there in the first place."

Moose grinned and mentioned the builder's name who had disclosed the secret location to him.

The sheriff smiled a little as he shook his head. "Why am I not surprised? That man couldn't keep a secret to save his own life." The smile faded as he asked, "I need to know one more thing. Did you take anything from that drawer, anything at all?"

"No," I said before Moose could. "Not a single thing."

The sheriff frowned at his hands for a moment before he spoke again. "So, you're trying to tell me that you stumbled across a pot of gold full of clues, and you didn't do anything about it?"

"We took some photos, and I recorded the message Sandy left him," I admitted.

"How did you manage to do that?" the sheriff asked, honestly interested in what I had to say.

"I took some photos with the camera in my phone," I said.

"I suppose you recorded the answering machine message with it, too."

I smiled at him. "I couldn't figure out how to do that."

"So then, what did you do?"

"I called my home answering machine and recorded it there," I said.

He nodded. "I'll give you credit. That was resourceful of you."

"Sheriff, I assure you that Moose and I didn't take a thing out of that drawer. We even left it open for you to find. Tell me you would have had a clue that it was there without us."

"We might have found it," the sheriff said grudgingly.

Moose wasn't having that. "We all know that's not true."

"I guess what I'm really asking is why you didn't call me when you found it," the sheriff said, and it was clear there was a hint of hurt in his voice. So that was why he was angry. Sheriff Croft wasn't necessarily upset that we'd found Barry Jackson's stash.

He was unhappy that we hadn't called him to tell him about it.

"I'm sorry," I said. "That was my fault."

"Victoria, it was our decision," Moose said, refusing to allow me to fall on my sword for the team.

"You should have called me," the sheriff said softly.

"We thought you would find it faster than you did, but that's no excuse," I said as contritely as I could manage. "We'll tell you everything in the future."

He looked at Moose, and my grandfather nodded. "We will."

That seemed to clear the air a little. "Good. Now tell me, what do you make of what you found there?"

He was actually asking us for our opinions on his case! I doubted he was just being polite; the sheriff wasn't known for his manners. He was clearly just as overwhelmed by the flood of suspects as we were.

"We have some theories," I admitted.

"There are plenty of those floating around," the sheriff said. "Would you care to be a little more specific than that?"

I looked at Moose, who nodded slightly, and I started to tell Sheriff Croft everything that we'd been thinking, including my latest theory that whoever had killed Barry Jackson had wanted his body to be discovered, the quicker the better.

"Who knew that a baker could cause that many folks to want to see him dead?" the sheriff asked after Moose and I finished filling him in on our theories.

"He seemed to have more than his share of enemies, didn't he?" I asked.

"It's hard to believe," the sheriff said. "So, what's next on your agendas?"

I wasn't about to hold back, not after the scolding we'd just received. I just hoped that my grandfather was okay with my disclosure. "We're going to talk to Mike Jackson, Rob Bester, and Cliff Pearson," I said. "Unless you'd rather we didn't."

"No, go ahead," the sheriff said.

"Seriously?" Moose asked.

"Why not?" Sheriff Croft asked. "I've already spoken with them all this morning, and no one was in the mood to talk to me at all. Maybe you'll be able to get something out of one of them that I can't."

I was about to say something when Moose cut me off. "We appreciate your confidence in us."

"One thing, though," the sheriff said seriously. "If you find out anything, no matter how small or insignificant it might seem to you, you share it with me, and I don't mean tomorrow or the next day, either. Got it?"

"We do," I said, and Moose nodded.

"Good. I'm glad we cleared the air," Sheriff Croft said as he stood. "Now if you'll excuse me, I have a pair of ladies to interview this morning."

"Good luck with them," I said, and then the sheriff left The Charming Moose.

My grandfather and I continued to sit there after he was gone.

"Can you believe what just happened?" Moose asked.

"Which part, the scolding or his willingness to let us dig into Barry's murder?"

"The scolding was expected, and don't think he's giving us a green light out of the goodness of his heart. He's stumped, Victoria. That's the only reason we're getting some room to operate here."

"I don't care why he's doing it, I'm just glad that we can dig without worrying about running afoul of the law."

Moose grinned at me. "Afoul of the law? Have you been reading Nancy Drew again?"

I laughed and swatted at him playfully. "Move over, you big lug. I need to take care of a few things here before we start interviewing suspects again."

"Happy to do it," he said as he stood. "Don't worry about coverage at the front. Martha's already on her way."

I smiled at my grandfather as I headed back to the kitchen to tell Mom what we were up to. Once my grandmother showed up, we could start digging into the murder a little more.

Hopefully this time we'd have a little more luck than we had so far.

But that was the thing about our investigations. No one

could predict what the final trigger was that revealed the killer's identity.

Until that moment came, we just had to do our best to ask as many questions as we could, follow every lead that came our way, and more important than anything, to stay alive.

Chapter 10

"I have an idea," Moose said as we left the diner half an hour later. "Since the sheriff has already spoken with the men we want to talk to today, why don't we approach our investigation from another angle?"

"I'm listening," I said. Sometimes Moose had great ideas that were just a little too unorthodox for ordinary law enforcement officers, but they almost always paid off whenever we pursued them ourselves.

"We need to speak with the people closest to our suspects before we tackle them again," Moose said.

"Do you mean like their family members?" I wasn't exactly sure how that was going to work, since, as far as we knew, Mike Jackson had lost his last remaining relative when Barry had died in the fire.

"No, I was thinking more along the lines of proximity," Moose explained. "We can try interviewing the business owners around Rob Bester's business, folks who live near Mike Jackson, and anybody we can come up with who might be doing business with Cliff Pearson."

"Moose, do you honestly believe that we could know anybody who might have anything to do with Cliff's business?"

"Victoria, people get in financial trouble all of the time. I've got a hunch that at least a few of our customers here at the diner owe Cliff money."

A sudden thought occurred to me. "You never borrowed money from him, did you?"

"Never," he said flatly. "I'm surprised you even had to ask."

"I'm sorry. I didn't mean anything by it," I said, quickly apologizing.

"Don't let it bother you," my grandfather said as he patted my hand. "As a matter of fact, I got into a tight spot when I first opened this place, and I'm ashamed to admit that I had to borrow from someone a lot worse than Cliff Pearson."

"Moose, you didn't," I said.

"I'm afraid that I did. Believe me, I was desperate when I went to Martha's dad and asked him for a short-term loan. It was one of the worst things I ever had to do in my life."

"Seriously? Why was that so bad? My great-grandfather was a warm and fuzzy puppy, at least what I remember about him."

"That's because he *liked* you," Moose said with a grimace.

"How could anyone not like you?" I asked with my broadest grin.

"I know, right? It never did make sense to me, either. After all, I'm a likeable fella."

I knew some folks in Jasper Fork who might disagree with that assessment, but I wasn't about to bring up any names. "Then again, you did marry the man's only daughter."

"True enough," my grandfather said. "It was sin enough in his eyes, that's for sure." Moose slapped his hands together and added, "Let's forget about my dark past and focus on our current investigation. What do you think of my idea?"

"I think it's golden, and for what it's worth, I fully approve of you," I said as I kissed his cheek.

"It's something I count on every day," he said with a smile as we left the diner in pursuit of new information about our pool of suspects.

"So, who do we tackle first?" I asked Moose as we got into his pickup truck.

"Well, the business folks we need to talk to might not be open yet," he said as he glanced at his watch, "and I'll have to make a few calls before I know who to tackle about Cliff Pearson."

"So Mike Jackson it is," I said. "I can't imagine anyone killing their own brother."

"Unfortunately, it's been happening since Cain and Abel," he said wistfully.

"Are you talking about your own brother?" I asked him as he drove to Mike Jackson's apartment complex. I had met my great uncle Martin only once, for my great-grandmother's funeral. As a matter of fact, I'd been startled as a child to find out I even had a great uncle.

"He was a terror to me growing up, and I swore that I'd have nothing to do with him once I was out on my own."

"What did he do to you?" I asked. Moose's voice had gone cold at the memory of past events. It was a side I rarely saw of my grandfather.

He thought in silence for the longest time, and finally Moose shook his head, as though he were trying to dispel bad memories. "Let's just say that my life has been a finer thing without him in it and leave it at that."

I knew not to comment further. My grandfather was devoted to his wife, his son, and me. He often said we were all the family he'd ever needed or wanted, and I took him at his word. Prying into his life with Martin wouldn't do anyone any good. "So, what are we going to do, just start knocking on doors and asking folks questions?"

"We have to be a little more subtle than that," Moose said.

I glanced at him and laughed. "I didn't think subtlety was ever your specialty."

"I didn't say that I knew how to go about it," my grandfather conceded. "I just think we need to come up with a cover story. You're good at that kind of thing. Do you have any ideas?"

"Let me think about it while we drive," I said.

"Well, think fast. We'll be at The Manor in a minute."

I considered different possibilities, and by the time Moose parked near the eight-unit complex on the outskirts of town, I had a plan.

"So, what's it going to be, granddaughter?"

"We're doing a background check on him," I said.

"For what purpose?"

"It seems that Mike Jackson has applied for a new job that requires a certain level of security."

Moose looked at me skeptically. "You've met the man. What kind of job could that possibly be?"

"I don't know, we'll probably need to be kind of vague. Do you still have that clipboard under your seat with the crossword puzzles on it?"

My grandfather reached down under his seat and brought it out. I saw the newspaper crossword puzzle on top was halfway filled out. It amused me for some reason that my grandfather had used blue ink to work it. That fact alone proved just how much confidence he had in himself. "Are you going to ask them puzzle questions?" he asked as he handed it to me.

I pulled the puzzles out and then rooted around in his dashboard for a minute.

"If you tell me what you're looking for, I might be able to help," Moose offered.

"This should do nicely," I said as I pulled out a few folded inspection sheets for the truck.

"How does that help?"

"These are going to be the forms we're using for our questionnaire," I said.

Moose laughed. "Okay. We can give it a try, but how are you going to explain our attire? We're both dressed a little casually for a pair of government workers, don't you think?"

"I'll cover that once we knock on the first door," I said, trying to show more confidence than I actually felt in my plan. I'd learned early on that if Moose and I acted as though we were entitled to do things, most folks went right along with us.

I just hoped that it worked this time.

"Hello, do you have a moment of time for us?" I asked as we knocked on the door beside Mike's apartment. "We're conducting personal interviews concerning your neighbor's job application."

The pretty young woman somewhere in her early twenties answered the door with a puzzled expression on her face.

"Why would you care about Mrs. Rosebaum, and who in their right mind would ever hire her? She's got to be eighty years old."

"Actually, this is regarding Michael Jackson," I said.

"The dead singer?" she asked, now even more puzzled than before.

"Your other neighbor," I said patiently, pointing to his door.

She nodded, finally putting the information together. "What do you want to know about him? Who are you, anyway?"

"We're with the government," I said.

"Okayyy," she replied, looking at my faded jeans and Moose's workboots.

"You've noticed our clothing, haven't you? Good. It's a new policy we're trying out to make people more receptive to speaking with us. On a scale of one to ten, one being completely uncomfortable and ten being happy to see us dressed this way, are you more or less at ease talking to us in casual clothing?"

"Five, I guess," she said, frowning still.

"Very good," I said as I pretended to note her response on the back of the truck's inspection form. "Now, about Mr. Jackson."

"What about him?" she asked.

"Is there anything you can tell us about him?" Moose asked, speaking for the first time.

"He hits on me a lot, if that's what you mean. The man won't take no for an answer."

"Tell us more," I said. If we could get her comfortable with us, we might be able to find out some things that Mike didn't want us to know.

"I mean, I guess he's cute enough, but he's like thirty or something. Ewww."

"Anything else?" Moose asked. I wasn't sure the girl could hear it in his voice, but I knew that my grandfather was getting frustrated. It was time to push her a little harder.

"We understand that his brother just died," I said.

The girl frowned again. "That's what Mike told me this morning. He came over and said that he was going to be rich. As if that would change my mind about him. Well, maybe it would. A little, anyway. How rich do you think he's going to be?"

"What made him think he was going to be rich?" I asked.

"He said he was inheriting a mint from his brother," she said.

"Did he mean the land the bakery was on?" Moose asked.

"No, apparently Barry had something else that was worth more than that, and Mike can't wait to cash it in."

This was brand-new information. It amazed me what men would say to impress women sometimes. "Did he give you any idea what it might be?"

"He said it was his brother's insurance policy, and now it was going to be his," she said.

I wasn't aware that Barry had carried any insurance. Was Mike just doing some hollow bragging, or was there something else that we didn't know about? "Did he go into any more detail than that?"

"No," she said. "I told him that I wasn't interested, no matter how much money he had. Maybe that was a mistake. What do you think?"

"You need to follow your heart," Moose said. "Is there anything else you'd like to share with us?"

She was about to speak when Mike Jackson's door opened. I hadn't counted on that, given all of the arrangements he had to make for his brother's funeral. He was clearly on his way out, but he stopped dead in his tracks when he saw us. "What are you two doing here?"

Before I could come up with a quick lie, the girl said, "They're here asking questions about you."

He frowned as he looked at her. "What did they want, Mindy?"

"They said you were applying for some big-deal job," she said.

"Well, they lied," he said. "Mindy, do me a favor and give me a minute with them, would you?"

"I don't mind at all." She started to go inside, and then she must have been having second thoughts about writing him off just yet. "When you're finished with them, I just made a fresh pot of coffee, Mike."

"If I have time," he said.

Instead of putting her off, that seemed to spark her interest in him, or his newly promised money, even more.

Once she was back inside, Mike said, "I don't know what you two think you're doing, but you'd better knock it off."

"We're trying to figure out who killed your brother," Moose said, the iron hard in his voice. "We'd think you'd want that, too."

"Of course I do," he said. "That doesn't explain why you're both poking your noses around my business, though, does it?"

"Mike, the sooner we can eliminate you as a suspect, the sooner we can get on with the rest of our investigation," I explained. "It's as simple as that."

"Well, let me save you both the trouble. I didn't kill my brother. Now go talk to someone else."

"But we're not finished talking to you," I said. "What's this insurance policy we're hearing about?"

He looked at the closed door of the apartment next to his. "Mindy often doesn't know what she's talking about, but that's never stopped her before."

"We weren't aware that Barry had any insurance," Moose said.

"I don't know if he did or not," Mike said flatly.

"That's not what you told Mindy," I reminded him.

"Yeah, well, I've said a lot of things to her over the past few months," he said. "She acts like she's not interested in me, but I know for a fact that she is. I thought if I hinted that I might be coming into some real money, she'd quit playing around." Mike glanced at his watch, and then he added, "I don't have time to stand around here talking to you. I'm late for an appointment."

"With Rob Bester?" I asked, taking a stab in the dark.

"No, as a matter of fact, I'm headed over to the funeral home to make arrangements for Barry's services."

I felt a little bad asking him such accusatory questions when he was going on that kind of mission, but our investigation couldn't wait.

"We won't keep you, then," I said.

Mike started to walk away when Moose called out, "We'll talk again later."

"I don't think so," he said as he disappeared.

Moose whistled softly under his breath. "That man's hiding something."

"I agree, but what?"

"In the spirit of cooperation, you need to give the sheriff a call."

"Why, to tell him about what Mindy said?" I asked.

"We need to find out if there's an insurance policy the police don't know about yet. It could be important, and besides, I'd really like to know."

I smiled as I pulled out my phone. "I wouldn't mind knowing that myself." I got the sheriff right away. "We just found out that Barry might have had an insurance policy, and Mike's the beneficiary."

"Where did you hear that?" he asked.

"Some girl named Mindy told us," I admitted. "Is it true?"

"Not that I've been able to uncover, and I've looked for one pretty hard," he said. "Have you gotten anything else that might be useful?"

"Hey, we just got started here," I said.

"Well, keep me in the loop," he said, and then the sheriff hung up on me.

"What did he say?" Moose asked me.

"He's not aware of any insurance policy Barry might have taken out, and he's been investigating it pretty thoroughly."

"So, was Mike telling Mindy the truth, or was he just trying to impress her?"

"I've got a hunch it was all for show," Moose said.

"Why do you say that?"

"You saw her too, right?" Moose asked with a grin. "It wouldn't be the first time a man lied to a pretty girl to gain favor with her."

"Have you ever done that in your long and seedy past?" I asked him with a grin.

"As a matter of fact, I never had to," Moose answered with a grin of his own. "So, should we talk to the famous Mrs. Rosebaum?"

"I don't see why not," I said as I moved over to her door and knocked.

Ten minutes later, we escaped with our lives. While Mrs. Rosebaum hadn't noticed anything amiss about Mike Jackson, she did share a litany of her aches and pains with us. The only way we got out of there was when Moose suggested she get a full body scan at the hospital, which she readily believed was a great idea. Two other tenants weren't home, or else they decided to ignore our knocks.

"Well, that was less than productive," Moose said as we got back into his truck.

"Hey, you know as well as I do that's what this business is about. You dig and dig, and most of what you uncover is worthless. That doesn't mean that you still don't have to do the legwork."

"I know. It's just that I had such high hopes for solving this case quickly. After all, we found all of the clues we've been going on early on in this investigation."

"For all of the good that it's done us," I said. "Do you think the businesses we need to visit are open yet, or should we track down some leads about Cliff Pearson's clients?"

"I don't see why we can't do both," Moose said. "Why don't you sit in the truck, and I'll make a few phone calls out here."

"Why can't I hear who you're going to call?" I asked. I hated being excluded from any part of our investigations.

"Because I don't want you to think any less of the folks I need to call in order to get more information. There's no reason in the world that you should think badly about any of our customers."

"Moose, I'm not that judgmental," I said.

"Victoria, I wish that I didn't know everything I do about some of our diners. Trust me, you don't want to know some of the sordid things that I know."

"Okay, I can see that," I said. He was right, too. I didn't want to treat any of our customers any differently just because I knew things about what they'd done in the past, for whatever reason. Maybe when I got to be Moose's age I'd be a little more forgiving than I was now. Besides, it was almost like a need-to-know basis, and I definitely didn't need to know everything that my grandfather did.

Moose talked for ten minutes, and I was about to wonder if he was ever going to finish when he finally hung up and got into the truck beside me.

"Any luck?" I asked.

"I have a few feelers out," he said. "We'll see what happens."

I couldn't get him to say anything more, though I tried.

"Then it's on to the businesses beside the burned-out bakery, then," I said. "Who knows? Maybe we'll have a little more luck there than we have so far."

"Where there's life, there's hope," Moose said with a grin.

Chapter 11

"You want to talk to me about Barry Jackson? Sorry, but I make it a habit not to speak ill of the dead," Jasper Jenkins said when Moose and I asked the plumbing supply shop owner about his neighbor.

"How about Rob Bester, then?" Moose asked. He and Jasper had known each other forever, and we'd decided, or more appropriately, my grandfather had decided, that he be the one who did the talking with Jasper. I didn't even fight him very hard on it. Jasper was on my bad side, and he had been since I'd been in the Girl Scouts. I could understand even then that not everybody liked our cookies, but when I saw him hiding inside as I rang his doorbell, he wouldn't even get off the couch to talk to me. Moose had gone back with me later and Jasper had bought some cookies after all, but it had left a bad taste in my mouth ever since, and whenever I saw Jasper waddling around town, I called him Cookie Man under my breath. I knew that it wasn't very mature of me. I was a grown woman, for goodness' sake, and yet I still held that particular grudge.

"He's as bad as Barry was," Jasper said.

I couldn't help myself. "Jasper, is there anybody in town that you like?"

"I can tolerate your grandfather in small doses," Jasper said.

Moose shot me a look, and I decided to go back to my silence and let him continue. Otherwise, I knew that I was going to snipe at Jasper about those cookie sales long ago, and that wouldn't do any of us any good at the moment.

"Talk to us, Jasper," Moose said. "We won't repeat what you say to anybody else."

"What do I care who you tell?" Jasper snapped. A few folks inside the store were shopping for plumbing supplies, but after a quick glance in our direction, they went right back to their shopping. After all, nobody wanted to get on

Jasper's bad side, as big as it was.

"You want to know the truth?" Jasper finally asked, lowering the decibel level of his voice a little. "They were the worst neighbors a man could have."

"Why is that?" Moose asked.

"When Barry first bought the bakery, he came around with a gift basket introducing himself. What a joke that was."

"I think it sounds nice," I said, despite Moose's earlier warning.

"Yeah? Well, I hate all those sickeningly sweet treats, but especially cookies. I thought you already knew that, Victoria."

I was about to respond when my grandfather reached out and grabbed my arm. After a moment to compose myself, I said, "It was still thoughtful of him."

"Maybe, but it was the first and last time he tried to get on my good side. When his bakery started doing poorly, do you know who he blamed? Me, that's who."

"Why would he do that?" Moose asked.

"Because I wouldn't let his overflow customers park in my lot. I even had one of them towed one time." The malicious smile on his face was downright creepy. "That taught him a lesson, you can bet that it did."

"So, what do you have against Rob Bester?"

"He thinks that he can buy my building just because he inherited some money from his grandpa. Well, I don't mind telling you, he's wrong!"

"He did?" Moose asked. "When did that happen?"

"Not more than a month ago," Jasper said. "I told him when he came sniffing around that he'd have to kill me to get my place, and you know what the man said to me?"

"What did he say?" Moose asked him.

"He told me right where you're standing that there were more ways to buy somebody out than going at them directly."

"What did he mean by that?" I asked, forgetting myself for a moment.

"He had the nerve to tell me that if I wouldn't sell, he knew someone who could give me a little nudge in the right direction," Jasper said.

"I bet that went over real well with you," Moose said.

"I told him that if he ever threatened me again, I'd make sure it was the last time he ever threatened anybody. I also told him that I don't make threats; I just make promises that I always keep."

"How did he take that?" Moose asked.

"How do you think he took it?" Jasper asked, that wicked smile reappearing for a moment. "That's when he left me alone and started going after Barry."

"How did the baker react to Rob's proposal?" I asked.

Evidently I'd gone too far. Jasper stared at me for a full ten seconds, and then he said, "If you want to know the answer to that, you're going to have to ask Rob. Now, if you two don't mind, I have a store to run, and a customer waiting to pay."

"That's okay, Jasper," Calvin Grishabor said. "Take your time. I'm in no hurry."

"Did anyone ask you for your opinion, Calvin?" Jasper asked.

Moose and I got the not-so-subtle hint. "Thanks for your time, Jasper."

"If I could think of a way to charge you for it, I would have done it a long time ago," Jasper said. He must have thought that he was the wittiest man ever born, because he started cackling insanely at his own joke.

I happily followed Moose out of the store. "That guy is seriously nuts," I said once we were on the sidewalk out front.

"He's not nearly as crazy as he seems to be," Moose said. "That always was his favorite act."

"Then he deserves an award for it if he's just pretending," I said. "The real question is can we believe what he just told us?"

"Victoria, Jasper ended up buying your cookies in the end,

remember? Don't you think it's time you dropped that particular grudge? It's not very becoming."

My grandfather had more beefs than the cattlemen's association, so he had a lot of nerve chastising me for one of mine. Then again, he was probably right. "Okay, consider it dropped. I just have one question for you, though."

"Fire away," he said.

"How exactly did you persuade him to buy those cookies?"

Moose frowned. "It wasn't my proudest moment, I'll tell you that."

"Now I want to know more than ever," I said. "Come on, share."

Moose sighed, and then he explained, "I told him that if he didn't buy your cookies, I'd make sure he wouldn't be eating anything that didn't come through a straw for a good long time."

"My hero," I said as I grabbed my grandfather's arm.

"I was a bully about it, and I'm not very proud of the way I behaved," Moose said, "but nobody crosses my favorite granddaughter, not then and not now, either."

I kissed his cheek as thanks, and then I pointed to Rob Bester, who was striding quickly toward us. "It looks like we've got some company."

"Good. I wouldn't mind chatting with Rob a little about all of this money he suddenly has."

"Don't you think he inherited it like he told Jasper?" I asked.

"I knew Rob's grandpa. That man never had more than two nickels to rub together his entire life. Wherever Rob got that money, it wasn't from Willie Monroe."

"So, how should we handle this?" I asked as Rob neared us.

"Let's just come out and ask him," Moose said.

"Ask him what?" Rob asked when he got close enough to us to have a conversation.

"Where'd you get the money you were trying to buy Flour Power with, Rob? And don't try to tell me that Willie left it to you. The man stayed dead broke all of his life."

"That's just what he wanted everyone to believe," Rob said with a smile. "He salted away half a million dollars over the course of his life, and he left every penny of it to me."

"Half a million? That's ridiculous. He wouldn't even buy his bread at the grocery store; it had to be at the outlet where they sold old cakes and pies."

"How do you think he saved so much? He never spent a dime of what he made if he could help it."

"I just don't believe it," Moose said.

"You can check with the courthouse if you don't believe me."

"Take it easy," Moose said softly, a hint of the danger to come if there ever was one. "There's no reason to get upset."

"Come on, boys, you're both pretty," I said as I stepped in between them. While it was true that Rob was quite a bit younger than my grandfather, Moose was still pretty wiry, and I'd never known him to back away from a fight. "Okay, Rob, that's wonderful that your grandfather was so thrifty, but that still doesn't explain why you want to buy the businesses on either side of you."

"So, you talked to Jasper about me, did you?" Rob asked me with a disgusted look on his face.

"It came up in our conversation," I said. Moose had backed off a few paces, but he still wasn't talking, which was maybe not all that bad a thing.

"I just bet it did," Rob said.

"It still begs the question of why," I asked him.

He waved a hand around him. "The honest truth is that I'm not satisfied with this little store," he said. "I want to tear it all down and build something truly spectacular."

"Just for selling tires?" Moose asked.

If Rob was offended by the question, he didn't show it. "Not just tires. I'm talking service bays for automobile repairs, and a new car lot on the other side. I'd be a full-service place, something that really mattered."

"Half a million wouldn't be enough to build those dreams," Moose said.

"Maybe not, but I could get a good start on them," Rob said. "Once I get the land the bakery was on, I'll be on my way."

"There's something else that you might not have considered," Moose said. "Mike isn't going to be able to sell you Barry's land until the murder case is solved."

"What makes you think that?" Rob asked my grandfather.

"Simple. It's because you can't profit from murder in this country," Moose said.

"But I didn't kill Barry Jackson," Rob said.

"Maybe you did, maybe you didn't. Who knows? But what if Mike did it? That would still tie up the land for next to forever."

"He didn't do it, either," Rob said, though he sounded a little less confident of it now.

"If he didn't, then who did?" I asked.

Rob looked to the left and then to the right before he spoke again. "There's someone else you haven't taken into account, someone with dark ties around town."

"Are you talking about the money Barry owed Cliff Pearson?" I asked sweetly.

Rob looked shocked that I already knew about his big revelation. "How did you know about that?"

Before I could answer, Moose said, "There's a lot we know about what's been going on around town lately, Rob."

"Yeah? Like what?" He seemed keenly interested in what my grandfather had to say, but if that was the case, his wish was going to go unfulfilled.

"If I tell you that, I might hamper the official investigation."

"Since when were you two official anything?" Rob said with a slight grin.

"As a matter of fact, we had a conference with Sheriff Croft at the diner about this case this morning," Moose said with a smug little smile.

"Well, either way, I'm not going to let it stop my plans," Rob said. "After all, I've done nothing wrong. If I can't expand my business here, perhaps it's time to pick up and move somewhere else."

"Maybe that's not a bad idea," Moose answered.

Rob looked around, and his gaze centered on the burned-out bakery. "You know what? The more I think about it, the better I like it. That could have just as easily been my shop burned to the ground." Rob shivered a little as he said it, and then he added, "I don't even want to think about that. Poor old Barry. He deserved better than what he got in the end."

"We can at least all agree on that," Moose said, and then he turned to me. "Come on, Victoria. We have more work to do."

"It looks like we got a hit," Moose said when he glanced at his phone as we got into his truck.

"What are you talking about?"

"One of my nibbles bit," Moose explained. "I've got a message on my phone from Sam Brody."

"What did he want?" I asked.

My grandfather looked at me before he started the engine. "Victoria, Sam borrowed money from Cliff Pearson, and he's willing to talk to us about it."

"Sam?" I asked incredulously. Sam Brody ran an ice cream place in town, and my husband, Greg, and I went there every now and then. I couldn't imagine the benign old man needing to borrow money from someone like Cliff Pearson.

"Sam," Moose confirmed. "Listen, he's willing to talk to us, but we can't be judgmental at all, okay?"

"Sure. That's fine with me," I said. "How did you know that he owed Cliff money?"

Moose tapped his temple. "It's truly amazing all of the things I know, young lady."

"I just bet it is," I said, smiling ever so slightly.

Moose started the truck, and as he pulled out, I asked him,

"Are we going to the ice cream shop?"

"No, he's not open today. He told me that he'd meet us at his house."

"What are we waiting for, then?"

As we drove to Sam's place on the outskirts of town, I asked Moose, "Why do you think Sam needed to borrow money from Cliff? Does he gamble? Or is it worse than that?"

"Does it really matter?" Moose asked.

"It does to me," I said.

My grandfather shrugged. "I don't suppose it will hurt to tell you. Sam's granddaughter needed an operation, and her folks couldn't afford it. Sam offered to pay, but the bank wouldn't let him take out another mortgage on his house or his shop, so he did the only thing he could think of; he went to Cliff."

"That's terrible," I said.

"What, that he borrowed money from a loan shark?"

"No, that his granddaughter needed an operation. How is she now?"

My grandfather grinned at me. "She's doing fine, the last I heard," he said.

"That's good. At least it was worth it."

"It's not up to us to say whether it was one way or the other."

I studied Moose a moment before I spoke. "You would have done the same thing for me, wouldn't you?"

"Victoria, there's nothing that I wouldn't do to make you well if you were sick, as long as it was in my power."

"Right back at you," I said with a smile. To my grandfather, and to me as well, our family was everything.

When we pulled up in front of Sam's place, my grandfather frowned.

"What's wrong?" I asked.

"That's not Sam's car," he said as we slowly got out of the truck.

"That's right," a voice said from the shadows of the deck.

"It belongs to me."

I looked at where the voice had come from and saw Cliff Pearson moving toward us, and from his expression, it appeared that he wasn't all that surprised to see us there at all.

Chapter 12

"You were expecting someone else?" Cliff asked us as he reached us. "Sorry to disappoint you."

"What are you doing here?" Moose asked him, taking a step forward as though he were trying to shield me from the loan shark. "Where's Sam?"

"What do you think I'm doing here? Sam called me, of course." I had some seriously dark thoughts about the ice cream man at that moment, but before I could speak, Cliff continued, "Don't blame him. It's one of the requirements that I ask of all my friends."

"Is that what you call your victims?" I asked him heatedly.

Cliff studied me for a moment before he spoke, and I could feel the anger radiate in the man's gaze. "I don't make anyone come to me. They all do it of their own free will."

"When there's nowhere else for them to go, maybe," I said.

"Then thank goodness that I'm there, right? Victoria, you just said it yourself. What would they do without me?"

"And you help them all out of the goodness of your heart, is that what you're saying?" Moose asked him pointedly.

"I'm a businessman," Cliff said with a shrug. "I deserve a return on my investment, just like a bank does."

"Maybe so, but I'm willing to bet that your return is a lot higher than theirs," I said.

"Have you ever looked at a bank's year-end report? They make me look like an amateur."

"We're not here to debate the morality of your business," Moose said. "We're looking for a killer."

"I told you before, I didn't kill anybody."

"And yet we don't believe you," I said. "Shocking, isn't it?"

"I've had about enough out of you, Victoria," he said as he raised one bony finger and pointed it straight at my heart.

I started to reply when Moose put a hand in the air. As

much as it went against my nature, I decided to keep my comments to myself, at least for now.

"Let's keep this civil, shall we?" Moose asked him. "Cliff, why are you here?"

"I told you to leave me and my business alone when you dropped in at the bowling alley. Surely you haven't forgotten our conversation so soon."

"We remember it," Moose said. "But that doesn't mean that we agreed to do anything you requested."

"I can see that," he said. "I'm a fair man, no matter what you two might think. I'm willing to give you one last warning to butt out. This is it. The next time you hear from me, it won't be nearly so pleasant for either one of you. Do I make myself clear?"

"We understand what you're saying. Now you need to listen to me. If you raise a finger against me, my granddaughter, or any member of my family for that matter, there's no place you can hide that I won't find you, and you won't like it when I do."

He shrugged slightly, and then Cliff Pearson said, "That's all that I came to say to you." He walked past us, and he was close enough for me to smell the expensive cologne he was wearing before he got into his car and drove away.

I hadn't realized that I was holding my breath until he was gone. "That was intense," I said.

Moose shrugged. "I've dealt with bullies before. The only way to respond to them is to not back down."

"What if he calls your bluff?" I asked my grandfather as we got back into his truck.

"Who said I was bluffing?" Moose replied, and we drove mostly in silence for a few miles.

If war had just been declared, I liked our odds. After all, we had Moose on our side, and that man was a force of nature, especially when he was angry.

I just hoped that it didn't come to that.

Our lives were, for the most part, peaceful and tranquil, and I hated the thought of anything intruding on that. Then again, I knew in my heart that Moose was right.

If we let one bully back us down from our investigation with a threat, then we might as well not even dig into the crimes that occurred around us.

And that was something that I absolutely would not stop, at least not as long as me, or any member of my family, was in danger in any way, shape, or form.

"Where are we going now?" I asked Moose.

"I thought we could swing by the diner," my grandfather said.

"I doubt that we're going to find any clues there," I said.

"Who said anything about looking for clues? I thought we might catch lunch."

It had been quite a while since breakfast, but we needed to solve this murder as soon as possible. "Can we really afford to take time off to eat?"

He looked at me askance as he drove. "Victoria, we're not going to be able to do ourselves any good at all if we're starving. Besides, I think better on a full stomach, don't you?"

"There's not much that I don't do better when I'm full," I admitted.

"So then, a quick bite it is."

"And after that?" I asked him.

"Then it's straight back to crime fighting, I promise."

It would be good to see Greg again, if only for a few minutes. I was spoiled, and I knew it. Most married couples didn't get to see each other during the workday, and that was one of the reasons that I loved running The Charming Moose. It didn't hurt that my husband was one of the best grill jockeys in the county, and that he was usually never more than a few steps away from where I was working.

"Okay, that should be acceptable. After all, I could eat something right about now," I conceded.

"That's my girl," he said, and a few minutes later, we pulled into the diner parking lot.

We didn't quite make it inside before someone approached us, though.

It appeared that lunch was going to have to wait after all.

"Sam, what are you doing here?" Moose asked the ice cream man as he approached us.

"I had to come by and apologize," the older man said as he looked at us in turn. "I didn't want to call Cliff, but I really didn't have any choice."

"It's okay, Sam," Moose said. "We understand."

"How's your granddaughter doing?" I asked him.

Sam glanced quickly over at Moose. "You told her?"

"It came up in conversation," my grandfather answered.

"I wish you hadn't said anything," Sam replied solemnly.

"Yeah, well, there are a lot of things that I wish for."

Sam just shrugged, and then he turned to me. "She's going to be fine. Victoria, I know what you must think of me, but I didn't really have any choice."

I leaned forward and kissed his cheek. "I think it's wonderful what you did for her."

Sam blushed a little from the attention, but he looked pleased nonetheless. "Well, I just hope that I can pay Cliff off soon."

"Is there anything we can do to help?" I asked.

"No, but thanks for offering. Anyway, I just wanted to tell you both that I was sorry."

Moose put a meaty hand on Sam's shoulder. "Don't worry about it. See you later."

"See you," Sam said, and then he left.

"I feel bad for him," I said after he was gone.

"He's a big boy, Victoria. He knew what he was doing when he called Cliff Pearson. I feel for him, too, but we can't take on his problems, or anyone else's. We've got enough of our own, don't you think?"

I nodded, and then I heard yelling coming from inside the diner. "What do you suppose that's all about?"

"I don't know, but there's only one way to find out," my

grandfather said as he pulled the door open and we walked inside.

The last two women on earth I would have expected to be in The Charming Moose were there. Well, that wasn't entirely true. I was sure that I could come up with an odder pair than the ones we found screaming at each other, but it was still a pretty odd couple. Sandy Hardesty and Susan Proctor, the two most recent women in Barry Jackson's life, were standing toe-to-toe yelling at each other at the tops of their lungs. Martha stood helplessly by watching them, and Greg looked relieved when we showed up.

"What's going on here?" I asked as I took my life into my own hands by stepping between them.

"Ask her," Susan yelled at me. "She's the one who started it."

"Me? What did I do?" Sandy asked loudly. "You're the one who interrupted my meal." The women were two studies in contrasts. Susan was in her mid-thirties, a lovely wisp of a redhead with pale, almost luminescent skin, whereas Sandy was easily ten years younger, a tall curvy blonde with warm blue eyes. How had Barry Jackson managed to attract these women? Personally, I didn't see it, and I thought each woman could do much better than they'd done choosing Barry.

I looked around and saw that they were attracting quite a bit of attention from our customers. "If you two can't keep your voices down, I'm going to have to ask you both to take this outside."

"Why should I leave?" Susan asked. "She's the one who started it."

"And I'm going to finish it, too," Sandy replied with fierce determination.

"Okay, ladies, let's go," Moose said as he gently put a hand on each shoulder. As he started walking them toward the door, I raced ahead and opened it for them.

Once we were all outside, Moose asked, "Now, what

seems to be the problem?"

Sandy pointed to Susan. "Ask *her*. She stole Barry from me, and now he's dead, so he'll never get the chance to realize what a mistake he made and come back to me."

"He could have lived a thousand years, and that still never would have happened," Susan said. "He got tired of being with a girl, so he decided what he needed was a woman in his life."

"An old woman at that," Sandy said snidely.

"At least I had more to offer him than a few curves and a girl's naiveté."

"What's that supposed to mean?" Sandy asked her.

"Look it up. It's in the dictionary."

"I know the definition of the word, you old hag," Sandy said.

"Then why did you ask me?" Susan asked. "You know what? I'm done with you. Suddenly I've lost my appetite."

"Go on and go, then. It's not like anybody's going to miss you."

Susan stared at her a moment, and then she started to walk off. On the spur of the moment, I called out, "Wait up, Susan. I'd like to chat with you a second."

I glanced back at Moose as I hurried to catch up to Susan and pointed him in Sandy's direction. Maybe he'd be able to get something out of her, if there was anything there in that shallow puddle of a girl.

"What do you want, Victoria?" Susan asked me impatiently. "I have to get to work."

"This will just take a second," I said.

"Go on, then," she said reluctantly.

"When Moose and I told you what happened to Barry, you had a pretty decent fire going."

"So what?" she asked.

"Were you burning anything more than branches and old paper?"

Susan looked at me oddly. "What business could that possibly be of yours?"

"I just found it curious, that's all," I said.

"That's going to get you into trouble someday, you know that, don't you?"

"What's that?"

"Your curiosity."

"Aren't you going to answer my question?" I asked her as she turned and walked away.

Evidently not.

Well, that had turned out to be a big bust.

Hopefully Moose was having more luck with Sandy.

When I got back to where I'd left them, I realized that the answer to that was probably not, since Sandy was gone, too.

"Well, at least we both struck out," I said as I rejoined my grandfather.

"What are you talking about?"

"Moose, don't try to tell me that you got more out of Sandy than I got out of Susan."

"Which was?" he asked.

"Nothing. Zilch. Nada."

"Then I managed to do a little better than you did," Moose said smugly.

"Tell me what you got," I asked.

"Sandy dropped a real bombshell before she left."

"What did she say, Moose?"

"She told me that a woman in Parker Ridge is claiming that she's pregnant with Barry's child. How's that for new information?"

"You're not serious," I said.

"I don't think Sandy was lying to me," Moose said. "This could change everything."

"No kidding," I replied. "Who is this mystery woman?"

"That's where it gets a little sticky," Moose said. "It's Natalie Dixon."

I had a sinking feeling in my gut. "Don't tell me she's related to Holly Dixon."

"I won't, but it's true nonetheless. Natalie is the judge's

granddaughter."

"We have to talk to her, Moose," I said.

"Don't you think I know that? Natalie could be our chief suspect now."

I looked hard at my grandfather. "I'm not talking about Natalie, and you know it."

"Oh, no," Moose said. "Don't even say it. My wife is still pretty upset with me that Holly came by the diner to see me."

"How about if I talk to Martha for you?" I offered. My grandmother might not kill me if I told her the news.

"No," Moose said as he took a gulp of air. "I'll do it."

It was one of the most courageous things I'd ever seen him do, and I'd watched him tackle an armed murderer before, so that was saying something.

"Do you want me to at least go in with you?" I offered.

"Tell you what. Why don't you go relieve her at the register and send her out here to me."

"Are you thinking she won't yell at you in public?" I asked him.

"Victoria, I've never known any set of circumstances that would keep your grandmother from doing anything she had a mind to do when she was angry. I just don't want anyone else to witness it if I can help it."

"Okay, if you're sure."

He gave me a weak grin. "As a matter of fact, I'm not, so you'd better go get her before I lose my nerve."

I touched his shoulder lightly. "Good luck."

"I'm afraid that I'm going to need it."

I waited to approach Martha inside until Gabriel Broome paid for his meal. Gabe nodded to me as he walked past, and my grandmother smiled brightly at me. "Victoria, I thought you already left when you didn't come straight back in." She looked behind me as she added, "Where's your grandfather? Isn't he with you?"

"He needs to talk to you outside," I said gently.

A frown creased her face. "What's he done now?"

"It's not so much what he's done as it is what he's about

to do," I said.

"I don't like the sound of that. Maybe you'd better tell me yourself."

"I would, honestly, but he wants to do it himself."

She took a step toward the door, and then she turned back to me. "Aren't you coming?"

"No, ma'am. I'm going to watch the front until you get back."

"Very well." She walked outside grimly, and I took up my usual position behind the register. As I stood there, I reached up and patted the wooden moose my grandfather had carved for me when I'd been a little girl. He was the diner's mascot, and I hoped that the luck he gave us extended to my grandfather outside.

He was going to need it.

Three minutes later, they walked back in together, though there was a noticeable distance between them. "Is everything okay?" I asked them.

"Why wouldn't it be?" my grandmother asked with a forced smile.

"No reason at all," I said quickly.

Moose shook his head, a clear signal that I should drop that particular line of questioning, but I didn't see how I could do it. Normally I did my best to stay out of the personal lives of my family, but this was directly related to a murder Moose and I were investigating, so I didn't feel as though I had any choice. "Martha, we have to do this."

"I know that, dear," she said. "That doesn't mean that I have to like it, though, does it?"

"If it helps, I'm going to be right there the entire time," I offered.

She patted my hand. "Don't you worry another second about it. Why do you think I agreed to let your grandfather go in the first place? Just keep an eye on him, okay?"

"I promise," I said as I kissed her cheek.

"Nobody needs to watch me, because I'm not going to do

anything I shouldn't do, okay?"

Martha turned and looked at him for a moment, and Moose quieted right down. She was the only person I'd ever met who could intimidate my grandfather into silence. It was a skill I wish I had myself sometimes, but I was pretty sure that if he were asked, Moose would say that he'd like the same ability to shut me up as well.

"Let's go, Victoria," Moose said.

"Can't it wait until we've had lunch?" I asked. I was really getting hungry now, and Parker Ridge was a good forty-minute drive away.

"We can pick something up along the way," Moose said. It was clear that he wanted to get out of there before Martha could change her mind.

"Nonsense," she said. "It won't take ten minutes, Moose. I know how intent you are on investigating this murder, but you both have to eat."

"Fine," he said as he pointed to a nearby booth. "Go ahead and sit down, Victoria. I'll go back to the kitchen and talk to Greg." Almost as an afterthought, he turned to Martha and asked, "Can I get something for you as well?"

"Thank you, but I'll eat later," she replied. There was just a hint of frost in it, but it was still enough to make my grandfather shiver a little.

Once he was gone, I spotted a slight smile on my grandmother's face. "I doubt that you're willing to admit it, but you're enjoying this, aren't you?"

"I'm sure I don't know what you're talking about," Martha said, and the smile quickly disappeared.

"Okay. Got it. I understand."

As my grandmother turned to go back to the register, she said softly to me, "Our men aren't always as clever as they think they are."

"To be fair, neither are we," I said with a smile of my own.

"Of course you're right," Martha said as she returned to my station and started cashing out patrons. I knew that my grandmother was not a big fan of Judge Dixon, not after her suspicion that the two of them had dated before she'd married Moose. Still, she was a rational woman, so there's no doubt in my mind that she knew the validity of our need to talk to the judge before we went off in search of her granddaughter. It was the right thing to do, especially if we ever wanted help from Judge Dixon in the future. Moose and I would have to tread lightly not to upset anyone we were about to question, but we couldn't just ignore what Sandy had told Moose. If Natalie was indeed carrying Barry's child, we needed to find out where she'd been the morning of the arson and murder.

Chapter 13

"I hope you're hungry," Moose said to me as he walked out a few minutes later carrying two plates barely able to contain enormous hamburgers and generous handfuls of French fries.

"I can't eat all of that," I said as I stared at the mound of food on the plate he slid in front of me.

"Then throw out whatever you can't hold," Moose said. "I, for one, plan to eat every last bite."

I glanced over at my grandmother, who was frowning at Moose's plate. "Martha's not very happy about your meal selection."

My grandfather lowered his voice and hid his smile from her as he said, "That's the beauty of her being angry with me. How much madder do you think she can get? I figured I'd indulge a little while the opportunity existed. After all, there's no reason not to take advantage of the situation, is there?"

"You're something else. You know that, don't you?"

"I sure do," he said, and then he took a big bite of his burger. "Man, your husband knows how to make a burger, doesn't he?"

"These aren't your creations?" I asked as I took a bite.

He shook his head. "No, ma'am. I wasn't about to intrude on another man's grill while he was cooking. It's just not done, you know?"

"Not really," I said. "Maybe it's some kind of short-order cook etiquette I don't know about."

"You'd better believe it is," Moose said, and then he took another bite, nearly sighing as he chewed and swallowed.

"If you eat all of that, you'll never make it to Parker Ridge without falling asleep," I said after I ate a few of the fries on my plate. Everything was delicious, but I wasn't really all that surprised. My husband could take just about any ordinary fare and make it into something special.

"If I start to nod off, I'll let you take the wheel," he said.

"No thanks. If something happened while I was driving that precious truck of yours, I'd never hear the end of it. After all, you've finally got it just the way that you want it."

"It's true, but I trust you with my life, Victoria, so why wouldn't I trust you with my truck?"

"Those are two very different things, and you know it," I said. A Southern man's truck was just about sacrosanct in his view, and I'd no sooner drive Greg's old truck as I would bump him from the grill and try to take over his cooking duties in back.

Some things were simply not done.

Once, long ago when we'd first been married, I'd borrowed my husband's truck to run to the bank when mine had been low on gas. I had his permission, but what I hadn't realized at the time was how reluctantly it had been given. There was a short bridge I had to cross before I got to the bank, and I wasn't used to driving up so high.

I hit one of the concrete posts.

It had kept me from going down into the small creek, and if I'd backed up, it might not have been so bad.

I panicked though, and muscled the truck on through, thinking that was the only way to get it unstuck.

That side panel was never the same, even after Greg had it repaired.

It was the first, and the last, time that I'd ever driven one of his vehicles, a hard-learned lesson.

"Yeah, you're probably right," Moose said as he polished off his burger and took a halfhearted stab at some of the fries still waiting for him. Pushing his plate away, he asked me, "Are you ready to tackle Natalie's grandmother now?"

"I'm as ready as I'll ever be," I said, taking one last bite, but still leaving half the burger on my plate. After all, I couldn't afford to have both of us going into food comas.

"Then let's go see the judge," Moose said as he put our plates and glasses in a nearby bin.

"The judge won't be free for five or ten minutes," the uniformed bailiff said at the courthouse. "You can wait over there."

"Sure thing, Lenny," Moose said as we took our seats on an ancient oak bench in the hallway outside the judge's chambers.

"What do you suppose she's doing in there right now, deciding a difficult case's final verdict?" I asked my grandfather softly.

"No, I'm willing to bet that she's on her lunch hour," Moose said as he glanced at his watch.

"I'd rather believe that she's in there weighing her next decision," I said.

"Suit yourself."

Four minutes later, the judge's door opened, and the bailiff walked into her chambers. He came out carrying a tray from the cafeteria a minute later, and Moose grinned at me. "Told you so."

I started to stick my tongue out at him in jest when Lenny turned to us and said, "You can go in, but you only have three minutes."

"We'll take it," Moose said, and we hurried into the tight room.

Judge Dixon looked surprised to see us. She was still in her robes, and she had an air of competence about her that suppressed most of her attractiveness, but not all of it. She was striking now even at her age, and I had to guess that she'd been lovely all of her life.

"What a surprise," she said as she looked at us from behind her desk. "What brings you two here? I doubt that it's a social call, since we just spoke so recently."

"Trust me, this isn't for fun, Holly," Moose said.

Before my grandfather could speak again, she interrupted him. "Moose, you know I don't stand on principle as a general rule, but if you could address me as judge while I'm robed and in my chambers, I'd greatly appreciate it. It's not for me. It's more out of respect for my office. Do you understand?"

"Completely," Moose said. "Judge, is it true that your granddaughter is pregnant with Barry Jackson's child?"

Holly was clearly stunned by my grandfather's question, and I nearly elbowed Moose for his lack of grace. The question had hit her like a fist in the gut.

"That's absurd on the face of it. I don't know what you're talking about. Tell me this instant, what have you heard?" she asked.

"That about sums it up, actually," Moose said. "Hol...Judge, if it's true, then that makes her a prime suspect in his murder."

The judge started to stand, the anger clear on her face, but after a moment's pause, she sat back down again, the fury now gone. It was an amazing thing to see, and I would have been in awe if I hadn't been so directly involved with the transition. "I need you both to step outside for a moment while I look into this."

"We need to..." Moose tried to say before I grabbed his arm and started pulling him outside.

"Take all of the time you need, Judge," I said. "We'll be waiting outside."

"Thank you. Shut the door behind you, if you will." It was clearly a command, an order that couldn't be refused. I would hate to ever stand in front of her during a trial, especially if I were guilty. Shoot, I was ready to confess now, and I hadn't even done anything.

The wait was considerably longer than the time Judge Dixon had promised us, but neither one of us was bound to complain. After a full ten minutes, the door opened again, and a robed finger beckoned us inside.

I didn't like the look of that, and I tried to prepare myself for the worst.

"Have a seat," the judge said, and Moose and I obeyed instantly. After we did as we were told, she moved back to her desk and faced us with a grim expression. "I just spoke with Natalie. She'll be here in one hour."

"We'd be happy to go there, Your Honor," I said. "We don't want to inconvenience her any more than is necessary."

"This isn't for anyone's convenience," she snapped. "Listen to what I'm about to tell you very carefully. You will not speak with my granddaughter unless I am present. Am I making myself understood?"

Moose frowned. "We're not trying to make her our scapegoat. We're just looking for the truth."

"I've made my decision," she said, giving Moose a look that expressed a lifetime of meaning. While I'd always thought that the judge still had a huge crush on my grandfather, she was protecting her own right now, and any fanciful thoughts she might have had about him were being subjugated by the instincts she was feeling about her granddaughter.

Moose started to reply when I tapped his leg lightly as I said, "Thank you, Judge. We'll be back in an hour."

My grandfather looked surprised by my total capitulation, but at least he waited until we were back outside of the judge's chambers before he spoke.

"I can't believe that you just caved in like that," Moose said.

"Did you honestly think that there was anything either one of us could say to make things better once she'd made her decision?"

Moose thought about it for a moment, and then he finally shook his head. "No, it was pretty clear that Holly's mind was already made up."

"That's what I thought," I said.

"So, what do we do in the meantime, just sit out here and wait for Natalie to show up?"

I looked at my watch. "No, I think we should go back to the diner."

"Didn't you get enough to eat before?" Moose asked incredulously.

"Of course I did. I'm going back so I can give Martha a break."

"What am I supposed to do while you're ringing up checks?" he asked.

"Oh, I don't know. Maybe you could spend a little time with your wife," I added with a smile.

"And get grilled about our meeting with Holly? No thanks. If I do that, I'm going to have to tell her that we're coming back again, too."

"She's not that scary," I said, chiding him a little.

"Says you," Moose answered, but he still followed me out to his truck. When we got to the diner, he pulled up in front but didn't shut off the engine. "I'll see you soon."

"Are you seriously not coming in with me?" I asked. "What am I supposed to tell Martha?"

"Tell her that I couldn't make it," he said.

I stayed right where I was. "You tell her yourself."

"Victoria, that would kind of defeat the whole purpose of not going in, wouldn't you say?"

I looked at him and tried my best not to grin as I asked my grandfather, "Are you really sure you want her to hear my interpretation of our earlier meeting?"

"But nothing happened," Moose said.

"So you say," I answered, now letting my grin show completely.

"Fine. You win." He parked the truck in a spot near the door, and we both got out. "You're more stubborn than I am; you know that, don't you?"

"I don't know that I'm more stubborn," I said.

"If you don't believe me, go ask your husband."

"Moose, he's been married to me long enough not to ever answer a loaded question like that."

As we walked in, Moose said, "I should have known. He's a smart man."

Martha looked surprised to see us back so soon. "That was quick."

"We have to go back in about an hour," Moose said.

As he started to explain, Martha said, "Save it, Moose. There's someone here to see you."

"Who wants to see me?" he asked as he looked around the crowded diner.

"Actually, he's here for Victoria, but he mentioned your name as well."

"What's this about?" I asked her as I scanned the room, too.

"He wouldn't tell me. It's the man in the three-piece suit over at that corner booth nursing a cup of coffee. I'd appreciate it if you'd see what he wants. He's taking up one of our best booths."

"I'll talk to him," I said as I walked toward him.

"I'll come, too," Moose said, and then he added apologetically to Martha, "Just in case."

"Go on," my grandmother said. "You and I will have plenty of time to talk later."

It was clear that Moose didn't like the sound of that, but at least for the moment, he'd won a temporary reprieve.

Now it was time to see what our visitor in the suit wanted from me.

"May I help you with something?" I asked the man as Moose and I approached his booth. I'd thought he was in his late fifties when his back had been to us, based on his thinning hair and his portly shape, but when I saw his youngish face, I lowered that estimate by half.

"Are you Victoria Nelson?"

Before I could reply, Moose stepped forward. "That depends on who's asking."

I gave him a nudge as I replied, "Please excuse my grandfather. Yes, I'm Victoria. And you are?"

He got out a business card and handed it to me. As Moose read over my shoulder, I saw that it said, "Thomas P. Graves; Holland, Sherman & Graves, Attorneys at Law."

"You're awfully young to be a partner in a law firm," Moose said.

"That's my father," the attorney said. Was that a bit of a blush on his cheeks? He must have gotten the question a lot, and it appeared that he hadn't found a way to easily answer it so far.

"What can we do for you, Junior?" Moose asked.

"Actually, I prefer Thomas, or simply Mr. Graves," the attorney said.

"Yeah, well I prefer a steak cooked perfectly medium, a wife who doesn't argue, and a fat wallet full of big bills, but the only one I get with any regularity is the first one on the list."

"Martha is standing right over there listening to you, you know," I said to Moose as I pointed at my grandmother.

Moose turned and shrugged sheepishly in her direction before he continued. "Mr. Graves, what can my granddaughter do for you?"

"I'm here to serve papers for you to appear in civil court for assault," he said as he tried to handle a legal document to me.

"Don't take it, Victoria," Moose said.

"I assure you, this is just a formality," the attorney said. "My client is ready and willing to pursue all legal avenues against you."

"When did this supposed assault take place, and who's making the complaint?" I asked.

"My client in this matter is Mr. Barry Jackson, as you'll see on that document," he said matter-of-factly.

"Mr. Graves, do you know that your client is dead?" I asked him.

"What are you talking about?" he asked, clearly unsure if we were joking or telling the truth.

"Pick up a newspaper, sport," Moose said. "Barry died in a fire at his bakery, so he's going to have a hard time suing us for damages."

This new information seemed to throw young Mr. Graves off his game. "Am I to believe your word in this matter?"

"Extra, extra, read all about it," Moose said as he grabbed

a nearby newspaper one of our customers had left earlier.

The attorney took the paper from my grandfather, began to read the headline, and then he abruptly stood. "I'll look into this promptly."

"You do that," Moose said to the attorney's retreating back. "That was easy enough."

"How do you know that he won't be back?" I asked, worried that Mike Jackson might change his mind and continue the lawsuit on his brother's behalf.

"He'll never win a civil suit unless we're found guilty in criminal court, and there's no way that case is ever getting prosecuted. Don't worry about him, Victoria."

"Moose, you know as well as I do that worrying comes with the territory when you run this place," I said.

He nodded. "I get it, but we have more pressing problems at the moment."

"Like Natalie Dixon," I said. "I'll try not to let Mr. Graves bother me anymore."

"That's the spirit. One problem at a time, granddaughter."

"That's true. This investigation seems to be supplying its own set of difficulties, isn't it?"

"Nothing we can't handle together, though," Moose said.

"You're awfully optimistic, aren't you?"

"Hey, it's the only way to be when things get tough."

I nodded, and then I walked over to my grandmother. "How would you like to take a break? I can't stay for much more than half an hour, but I can at least relieve you that long."

"I'm fine, dear," she said. "Go spend it with your husband."

"I really don't mind," I replied. "I can catch up with Greg tonight. Go on. I insist. Why don't you get Moose to sit with you, and I'll take your lunch order myself?"

"Well, I could use a bite to eat," she conceded. "Are you sure?"

"I'm positive," I said.

"Excellent, but you stay at the register. I'll let Moose

fetch my food for me."

"Yeah, that probably is better," I said with a smile.

She winked at me before she joined my grandfather. I loved the way that the two of them interacted, but I was glad that Greg and I had less drama in our married lives than they did. I knew that he'd understand my decision to relieve my grandmother instead of visiting him in the kitchen. If anything, my husband was more into our family than I was, and that was saying something.

For the moment, I just wanted to get lost in my work and forget all about arson and murder.

After all, our appointment with Natalie and her grandmother would be happening soon enough.

Chapter 14

"It's time to go, Victoria," Moose said as he approached the register and tapped his wristwatch.

"Give me one second," I said as I finished ringing up Penny Winston's ticket. "Have a nice day, Penny," I said as I handed over her change.

"Right back at you," she replied.

I looked over at Martha after Penny was gone. She noticed the attention, stood, and joined us at the register. "Thanks for the break, Victoria."

I hugged her. "Thank you for filling in for me," I said.

"It's honestly my pleasure," she replied.

"The clock's ticking," Moose said softly in my ear.

"Okay, okay. I'm ready."

Once we were outside, Moose said, "Thanks for abandoning me, by the way. Why didn't you take Martha up on her offer to watch the front while you spent a little quality time with your husband?"

"I figured that the two of you had a few things to talk about," I said with a slight smile. "Was I wrong?"

"Well, I don't know how much talking I did, but Martha surely got enough words in for the both of us. It's amazing to me that she had any time left over to eat."

"She's had a lot of practice scolding you over the years," I said. "There's no doubt in my mind that she could do that on autopilot."

"You're probably right, not that I haven't deserved it most of the time."

"*Most* of the time?" I asked him as he drove toward the courthouse for our appointment.

"Okay, nearly all of it. Is that better?"

"Much," I said as he parked in the lot and we made our way inside. I wasn't expecting open arms when we arrived, but I did think that the door to the judge's chambers would at least be open. Instead, we found Lenny there again, guarding it like a watchdog.

"Is she ready for us?" Moose asked as he started to reach for the handle.

"No," the bailiff said as he continued to block our way.

"Is there a problem?" I asked him lightly.

"Not as far as I'm concerned. I'm just doing as I've been told."

"Good for you," Moose said, the irritation thick in his voice. "Just exactly how long are we supposed to hang around here waiting?"

"I personally don't care if you leave right now," the man said. "All I know is that you're not getting through this door until the judge says it's okay."

There didn't seem to be a lot of room for debate, so I guided my grandfather back to the bench we'd so recently occupied together, and we both sat down.

"If I'd known she was going to pull this, I never would have left in the first place," Moose said a little sullenly.

"This is no time to jump to conclusions. We have no idea what's going on back there."

My grandfather shook his head. "Victoria, if Holly isn't back there talking to Natalie at this very moment, I'll buy you a brand-new hat."

"I don't wear hats, and you know it," I said.

"It's just an expression."

"Really? I've never heard it before." I leaned over and asked Lenny, "Have you ever heard of that?"

"Not even once," the bailiff said, proving to me that he was indeed eavesdropping on our conversation. It might be wise for us to watch what we said in his presence. There was little doubt in my mind that Lenny would tell Judge Dixon everything that my grandfather and I discussed while we were waiting for her summons.

Moose said sullenly, "Well, I've heard it plenty of times."

"I'm sure that you have," I said, trying to mollify him.

It didn't work.

He was as impatient as a child going to an amusement park, and I wondered if the door would ever open, when finally, the handle turned, and the bailiff stepped aside.

After a whispered conversation, he turned to us and said, "You can go in now."

It was showtime.

Soon enough, we'd find out what all of the secrecy had been about, and if we got lucky, maybe we'd learn one way or the other if Natalie Dixon was really carrying Barry Jackson's baby.

There was an attractive young woman sitting in the chair that Judge Dixon had pulled up beside her own, and it was clear in more ways than one that battle lines had been drawn. The massive desk separated Moose and me from the two Dixons, and I wondered if this was going to be the start of a new family feud.

"Moose, Victoria, I'd like you both to meet my granddaughter, Natalie," the judge said formally.

Moose and I shook hands with her as she stood, and the beginning signs of pregnancy were clearer now. I'd known Barry Jackson for years, and I'd never found him to be all that charming, let alone attractive. So how had he been able to woo this particular young lady? I desperately wanted to know, but it wasn't a question that I could just come out and ask.

After the introductions were made, the judge said, "Before you start asking questions, Natalie would like to say something first, if there aren't any objections."

I couldn't imagine there being any, and I was proud of Moose for remaining silent. "Please go on," I said, and Judge Dixon nodded, adding the grim hint of a smile.

When her granddaughter didn't speak up right away, the judge looked at her and said, "Go on, Natalie. Tell them what you told me earlier."

"I can't," the young woman said, nearly breaking down in tears. "It's too embarrassing."

"Nevertheless, it needs to be done," Judge Dixon said. To soften the harshness of her demand, she reached over and patted her granddaughter's arm gently. The treatment of her kin was just like I imagined her demeanor in court must be, firm but fair.

"Okay," Natalie said as she turned toward us. "I would never sleep with Barry Jackson, and there's no possible way that this is his baby," she said in a rush of words. The young woman looked at her grandmother, and the judge nodded, her smile obvious now.

"Tell them why you said what you did," Judge Dixon said.

Natalie moved her gaze to the hands in her lap as she said, "My folks have hated my boyfriend from the start, and my dad threatened to kill any man who got me pregnant before I was married. When I found out I was pregnant, I'd just been to the bakery. I panicked when my father asked me who had done this to me, so I said it was Barry."

"What happened next?" I asked softly.

"My dad went to the bakery and accused Barry Jackson of knocking me up," she said. "Barry was there with his ex-girlfriend at the time. Evidently she was trying to patch things up with him. Anyway, Dad confronted Barry, and before long there was an ugly scene. My mom managed to drag Dad off, but not before he told Barry that he'd be back for him."

Moose said, "Sandy never told me about that part of it."

Natalie spoke up. "She probably didn't know about it. Dad said she took off the second he showed up. She's not exactly brave, at least according to him."

"I hate to ask you this, but do you know where your father was the morning the bakery burned down?" I asked her.

"My son has many flaws, but he's not a killer," Judge Dixon said firmly.

"Pardon me for saying this, but we aren't always the best judges of our own children's behavior," Moose said.

"Perhaps not, but the morning in question my son happened to be sleeping on my couch."

"He and Mom had a huge blowout fight about me," Natalie said. "I tried to get them to stop fighting, but Dad left before I could set things straight."

"When that happened, he came home to me," the judge said, "where I scolded him for his behavior, and then I made a space for him on my couch. I have a perfectly good guest room, but I didn't want him to get too comfortable there. I've taught my son to face his problems, no matter how dire they might seem, and I wasn't about to go back on that belief. He wouldn't tell me what the fight was about at the time, but it's clear enough now, isn't it? In any case, there's no way that my son could have been involved with whatever happened to Barry Jackson on the morning of the fire. You have my word on it."

"That's good enough for me," Moose said, and I wasn't about to dispute it.

"How are you holding up, Natalie?" I asked her.

"I'll be all right," she said. "I'm not looking forward to the next hour, though."

The judge said, "My son and his wife are on their way over here, and Natalie is going to tell them the truth. We're going to clear the air, once and for all."

There was a knock on the door, and the bailiff stuck his head in. "I'm sorry to interrupt, Judge, but he's here."

She nodded, and Lenny stepped aside, allowing a young man inside the cramped quarters. The second he was there, he rushed to Natalie and embraced her. "Are you okay?" he asked gently.

"I'm fine," she said. "What are you doing here, Jarod?"

"I called him," the judge said. "It's high time that there are no more secrets in this family."

"But I'm not a part of your family," Jarod said. "Your son has made that clear time and time again."

"Young man, my granddaughter is carrying your child," the judge said. "That makes you family."

It was time for us to leave. "If you'll excuse us, we'll be on our way," I said as I stood.

The judge said, "Natalie, Jarod, would you both mind waiting out in the hallway for one minute?"

Natalie looked terrified by the prospect. "What if Mom and Dad come?"

"Don't worry. Lenny will be right there to keep the peace," she said.

They agreed, and after the young couple was gone, the judge said, "I trust this ends my family's involvement in your investigation."

"I said that it did," Moose replied. "You know that you can trust my word."

"I do," she said, and as she said it, her calm demeanor slipped for just a second, and I could see the woman beneath it. "This is a trying day for all of us."

"I know that you'll handle it like a pro, Holly," Moose said softly, and she didn't even chastise him for not calling her judge.

She nodded her thanks to us both, and then Moose and I left.

We said our good-byes to Natalie and Jarod in the hallway, and then Moose and I made our way back out to his truck.

"I wouldn't want to be any of them in an hour," Moose said. "There's no one that it's going to be easy on."

"Life can be sticky sometimes," I said, "but with the judge there, I think they'll all be okay. She's a tower of strength, isn't she?"

"She can be, but sometimes I worry about her," Moose said.

I was glad Martha hadn't heard him say that. "Why?" I asked softly.

"Never mind," my grandfather said, dismissing my question. "Now that we've settled that, we can get back to our investigation."

"That sounds good to me, but where do we go from here?" I asked. "We've spoken with all of our suspects today, and there's nothing new that we can ask any of them until we get more information."

"Then I suppose the only thing that's left is to head back to the diner," Moose said. "Don't worry. I'm sure something will turn up."

It did, too, before we even got back to The Charming Moose.

As we were driving, a police siren went off behind us, and I looked back to see flashing lights following us closely.

It appeared that Sheriff Croft had grown tired of waiting for us to report back to him.

"Don't tell me you're going to give me a ticket for something," Moose said as the sheriff walked up to his side of the truck. "I know for a fact that I wasn't speeding, and I just had this thing inspected at the garage. Wayne gave it a clean bill of health."

"This isn't about your truck," Sheriff Croft said. "I didn't know how else to get your attention. I tried flashing my headlights, but you ignored me."

"I thought you were just one more lunatic trying to run me off the road," my grandfather said.

"You might not be that far off," the sheriff said. "We need to talk."

"Why don't you follow us back to the diner?" Moose suggested. "We'll all be a lot more comfortable there, I can promise you that."

"Sounds good," the sheriff said. "I could use some pie."

"I'm always in the mood for that," I said. "We'll see you there."

As he walked back to his squad car, I asked Moose, "Did he seem to be in a particularly good mood just now?"

"For him, he was practically doing cartwheels," Moose said.

"I wonder what's up?"

"I'm trying to figure out if he's even going to tell us," my grandfather said. "Maybe there's been a break in the case."

"If there has been, it's not because of us. This thing

started out so promising when we found all of those clues at once, but we've just hit dead end after dead end ever since."

"You know as well as I do that there's no predicting how these things are going to work out," Moose said. "Maybe this is going to be one of those times where the sheriff beats us to the punch and solves the case without us."

"To be honest with you, I wouldn't even mind that happening," I said. "I'm willing to bet that there are several folks around town who think that we killed Barry to stop his lawsuit against us, and they aren't going to change their minds until the real killer is found."

"Victoria, I taught you long ago that you can't worry about what other people think of you."

"That might work in the schoolyard, but in real life, things don't always work out that way," I said. "If our reputation is tainted by this, we might lose some of our customers forever."

"If they feel that way, then I say good riddance."

"Easy for you to say. You're not responsible for the bottom line anymore," I reminded him. "If you wanted to, you could move up to your fishing cabin and forget all about The Charming Moose."

"I think your grandmother might have something to say about that," Moose said.

"Who knows?" I asked with a grin as we pulled up at the diner. "She might even encourage it."

"You talk that way now, but you'd miss me if I were gone," he said lightly.

I suddenly realized how I must have sounded. I cherished my grandfather, and while I knew in my heart that I wouldn't have him with me forever, the prospect of ever losing him was one that sobered me instantly. "You know that I love you, right?" I asked before we got out.

He looked startled by my confession, but in an equally somber voice, he answered, "I love you, too."

Hearing it made me suddenly feel better.

"Then let's not keep Sheriff Croft waiting," I said with a

smile.

"We can't have that, can we?" Moose asked with a grin of his own. "How's he ever going to solve this case without us?"

"I don't know that we've helped all that much so far," I said.

"Hey, we found the original clues in this case, remember? We may not have been able to do much since then, but without that secret drawer discovery, we'd all be flailing around in the dark."

"That's true enough," I answered. "Maybe it's time for the sheriff to add something to the investigation."

Moose winked at me. "Why don't you tell him that once we get inside?"

"I don't think so," I replied, wondering what we were about to hear.

Chapter 15

"Moose, why don't you join the sheriff while I get us all coffee and pie," I told my grandfather as we walked into the diner. Sheriff Croft had already chosen a booth away from the few other diners we had at the moment, and I signaled to Jenny that I'd take care of them myself. Moose and I had burned most of the afternoon dealing with Natalie Dixon and her own particular set of woes, and Ellen had left long ago.

I popped into the kitchen for the pie and gave my husband a quick kiss as he worked the grill.

"Hey there, stranger," Greg said. "You've been busy today, haven't you?"

"It seems like it, but we haven't gotten much accomplished," I said as I collected three slices of Greg's Dutch apple pie and put them on a tray.

"Well, at least there's pie," Greg said. "Who's the third piece for?"

"The sheriff wants to talk to us," I said. "He's already out there with Moose."

Greg flipped a towel at me and grinned. "Well then, you'd better get out there. You don't want to miss anything."

"You're right," I said, "as much as I'd love to hang out back here with you."

"Don't worry about that. There will be plenty of time for us later," he said. "Now shoo."

I did as he said, grabbing a coffee pot on the way.

The two men were already in earnest conversation, and as I filled three cups with coffee, I asked, "Did you two get started without me?"

"Just some of the preliminaries," Moose said.

"Well, isn't that a shame," I said as I slid a piece of pie in front of each man, holding one out for myself.

"Why's that?" the sheriff asked.

"You're just going to have to start all over again now that I'm here," I said with my brightest smile.

"Victoria, it was nothing, really," Moose said.

"Then it shouldn't be that hard catching me up," I replied.

Moose looked at the sheriff and shrugged. "I told you we should have waited."

Sheriff Croft sighed once, and then he said, "Okay, to recap, here's where we are so far. After your grandfather brought me up to date on what you two have uncovered, I was just about to tell Moose that we've been able to eliminate two of our mutual suspects."

"Two? How did you manage that?" I asked.

"Well, I'm the first to admit that it doesn't hurt having official status investigating, plus, our resources are much broader than yours. You shouldn't be discouraged by what we've uncovered."

I smiled at him. "Discouraged? You misunderstood my reaction. I'm elated that we're going to be able to strike two names off of our list. Who have you eliminated so far?"

The sheriff lowered his voice, and then he said, "This is just between the three of us, agreed?"

"We promise," Moose said.

I echoed the sentiment.

"Okay then. Cliff Pearson is off the hook, unless he paid someone else to torch the bakery, which I find highly doubtful."

Drat. He was one of my favorite suspects. "How can you be sure?" I asked him.

"Evidently, at the exact time that the bakery was being torched, Cliff was being tailed in Charlotte by the police force there. It seems that he has been branching out from our area in an attempt to hit the big leagues, and he's come to the attention of the Charlotte Police Department."

"Are they sure it was him?"

"It's a positive ID," the sheriff said. "I'm fully confident in it."

"Like you said, though, he still could have paid someone to do it for him," Moose said.

"That's possible, but doubtful. Evidently Cliff prides

himself on being a hands-on criminal. He's even broken a few legs of delinquent clients himself."

"Who else have you been able to mark off your list?" I asked him.

"Susan Proctor was just getting back from a business trip when Barry was murdered," he said.

"She could have come back here earlier to do it," I suggested.

"Not from Seattle. Her plane landed at Charlotte Douglas Airport ten minutes before the fire started, and it's an hour and a half drive from there to here. We got confirmation that she was on that exact flight."

"Why didn't she tell us that earlier and save us all a lot of trouble?" I asked.

"Evidently the meeting was a job interview, and she didn't want anyone to know that she was looking for something else. That woman was more afraid of losing her current job until she secured a new one than she was in clearing her name of murder."

I remembered the fire she'd been burning when Moose and I had visited her, and how certain I'd been that she was covering up the smell of smoke on her from something more nefarious.

"You look disappointed now, Victoria," the sheriff said.

"I kind of had my hopes pinned on one of those two," I admitted. "Cliff made sense because of his background, and Susan was burning things in a trash can by her house when we went to see her the afternoon of the fire. I was positive she was covering something up."

"Well, it often works out that way. We don't usually get our killers wrapped up in nice little packages," Sheriff Croft said.

"Then that leaves us with three amateurs," Moose said. "Unfortunately, they each have their own motives for murder."

"It's awfully cold blooded, killing Barry and then starting a fire to hide what they'd done," I said.

"Who knows if that's why it even happened? The entire thing could have been done out of sheer panic," the sheriff said. He was about to add something to his comment when his radio went off. After a whispered conversation, he said, "I've got to go. Somebody just broke into the mayor's storage shed, and he's ready to mobilize the National Guard."

"Can he do that?" I asked.

"Not a chance, but I've got to get over there before he tries."

After the sheriff was gone, I turned to my grandfather. "He just took away my favorite two suspects."

"I know. I liked them both myself."

"So now we have Barry's brother, his old girlfriend, and a man who wanted to buy his property at any cost. The bad thing is, any one of them could have done it."

"Then we need to dig a little deeper and find out which one it was," Moose said.

"I'm not disagreeing with you. I just don't know how to go about it."

My grandfather glanced at the clock. "We don't have a lot of time left this evening anyway. Why don't we both sleep on it and compare notes again in this morning? We're not going to be able to solve this case tonight; that's for sure."

"I wish I could argue with you, but I'm fresh out of ideas. Go ahead and take Martha home. She deserves a break after the day she's had, and I'll take over here."

"That sounds like a plan," Moose said as he stood. "Don't worry. Something will come to us."

"I hope you're right," I said.

After my grandparents were gone, I told Jenny she could take off early.

"Are you sure?" she asked even as she headed for the door.

"Positive," I said with a laugh, and then she was gone.

After I topped off a few teas and coffees, I ducked into the kitchen for a second. "I sent Jenny and Martha home. It's just the two of us now."

Greg grinned at me. "We only have ten minutes left that we're going to be open. I think we can handle it. Should I make us something to eat?"

"That would be glorious. Let me throw the last few diners out, and we can start now."

He laughed. "I'm not going to tell you how to run your business, but I can wait ten minutes if you can manage it."

"I know in my heart that you're right," I answered with an exaggerated sigh. "I just don't have to like it. Ten minutes it is."

"Don't worry, it will fly by."

It didn't, but I wasn't about to hold that against my husband. Finally, after what felt like forever, I was about to lock the door behind our last customer when Cass Hightower came rushing up to the door.

"Are you closed yet?" he asked.

"Sorry, you just missed the cutoff," I said. Cass was a huge gossip, a man notorious for ordering a cup of coffee and a piece of toast and making them last for hours while he regaled anyone who would listen with his latest lies and rumors.

Cass frowned, and then he suggested, "How about if I get it to go?"

I thought about it for a second, and I realized that I really didn't want Cass adding any stories about us to his mix of tales. "It's got to be Greg's choice, but I'll give it to you half-off if you take whatever he makes for you," I said.

I suspected that Cass's tightwad tendency would overrule his sense of taste, and I was right. "You've got yourself a deal," he said.

Reluctantly, I let him in, and then I locked the door behind him. "Sit right here and wait for me," I said, and Cass did as he was told.

When I came back into the kitchen, Greg said, "See? That wasn't so bad."

"You're not finished yet," I said. I explained the deal I'd made with Cass, and my husband grinned.

"I'll make him a turkey sandwich. He *hates* turkey."

"We don't want to alienate him if we don't have to," I gently reminded my husband.

"I was just kidding," Greg said. "I'll fix him some chicken soup and make him a quick grilled cheese sandwich. When he orders more than toast, that's almost always what he gets."

"You're a good man," I said as I kissed my husband's cheek.

"Maybe I just act that way when you're around so you'll think so," he said as he started on the sandwich.

"Then I'm happy to tell you that it's working," I said. I ladled some soup into one of our to-go bowls and put a lid on it. "How long until the grilled cheese is finished?"

"An artist can't hurry these things," Greg said.

"How about you, though?" I asked with a smile.

"Give me two minutes. I'll bring it all out when it's finished."

"That's a deal."

I went out front to find that Cass was no longer sitting where I'd told him to be. Instead, he had his back to me and was staring out the window.

"Is everything okay, Cass?" I asked him as I approached.

I must have startled him, because he practically jumped out of his skin when I finally got his attention. "You just about gave me a heart attack, Victoria."

"What's going on out there?" I asked as I looked over his shoulder.

"I thought I saw someone in the shadows across the street watching me," Cass said as a shiver ran through him.

"Why would someone be watching you?" I asked. "What have you been up to lately?"

"Not a thing. That's what's got me so perplexed. It's creepy, you know?"

"The darkness can play tricks on your eyes," I said. "I'm

sure that it's nothing."

Cass didn't look all that convinced, but he nodded anyway. "So, what's Greg making for me?"

"He mentioned a turkey sandwich," I said.

"I hate those things," he said. "Please tell me that you're kidding."

"I am," I said. "He's making you a grilled cheese and chicken soup combo."

"That's fine, then," Cass said.

"Why the loathing of turkey?" I asked as I rang up his halved bill, and he quickly paid.

"When I was a boy, my grandmother kept live turkeys in the yard. She called them Thanksgiving and Christmas, since that's when she ate them. It was tradition in her family, one that she could trace back to the Civil War. Anyway, one year she had a tom that was extremely aggressive, and he'd come after me anytime I was near. It got to the point where I couldn't even visit her. Ever since, I can't stand being around anything even remotely turkey-related."

"I'd think you'd want to eat them every chance you got to get your revenge," I said.

"Sadly, it never worked that way," Cass reassured me.

As I gave him his change, Greg came out carrying a large bag. "Here you go, Cass."

"Thanks, Greg," he said, and after he took possession, I let him out and locked the door behind him. I lingered there to see if anyone from the shadows emerged, but if someone had been out there in the first place, they didn't follow Cass down the road.

"What's going on?" Greg asked as he looked out as well.

"Nothing. Cass thought he saw someone lurking in the shadows."

Greg looked a little harder. "I don't see anyone. Should I call the sheriff?"

"No, I'm sure that it was nothing more than Cass's overactive imagination," I replied.

"I don't know. You can't take chances like that when

you're investigating a murder." Greg reached for his phone, and before I could stop him, he'd dialed 911.

"Sheriff, could you send someone past The Charming Moose? We might have someone watching us in the shadows from across the street."

After my husband hung up, I said, "You didn't have to do that. It's probably nothing."

"It can't hurt," Greg said. "After all, if something were to ever happen to you, I'd never be able to find someone else anywhere near as willing to put up with my nonsense."

"And I'd hate the thought of training someone new myself. Look how long it's taken me to civilize you."

He wrapped me up in his arms, and I felt the safety and love he radiated toward me. "That's so sweet. I love you, too, Victoria."

Two minutes later, a squad car came by, and it slowed as it neared the diner. A powerful searchlight swept the shadows across the street, but nothing seemed to be out of the ordinary. The interior light of the squad car lit briefly, and one of the deputies waved to us.

We waved back, and he disappeared.

"See?" I asked. "It was nothing."

"Or whoever was there had enough sense to move on before someone caught them," Greg replied.

"My, but you're sounding particularly paranoid tonight," I replied.

"Like I said, I don't want anything to happen to you."

"Or me to you," I said. "So, what's for dinner?"

"Well, call me crazy, but all of this talk about turkey made me crave some. I've got two plates with turkey, stuffing, mashed potatoes, green beans, and cranberry sauce. Interested?"

"As a matter of fact, that sounds great."

As we ate in the back, I took the first forkful of bird and held it up in the air. "To Tom Turkey," I said.

"To Tom," Greg repeated, and we shared a wonderful meal together.

By the time we left the diner, I had forgotten all about the possibility that someone might have been lurking in the shadows watching us.

Later that night, though, it was the first thing I thought of when Moose called me.

The bedside clock read 2:37 when I answered the phone, so I knew that my grandfather wasn't calling me to discuss the weather, or even our future plans for our investigation.

If the time of night hadn't been enough of a giveaway, then his tone of voice would have done it all by itself.

Moose had a serious problem, and my grandfather was about to dump it right into my lap.

Chapter 16

"Somebody just lit my truck on fire," Moose said wearily after I picked up the phone.

"What? Are you okay?" I asked sleepily.

"What's going on?" Greg asked me.

"Hang on," I told him.

"Okay," Moose replied.

"Not you, Greg. Now tell me what happened."

"I had a dream that I was in the middle of a forest fire," Moose said. "When I woke up with a start, I noticed that it was lighter out than it had any reason to be. One glance out the window and I saw that my truck was in flames. I ran downstairs in my nightshirt as Martha called the fire department. Good thing I had a heavy-duty fire extinguisher handy."

"Were you able to put it out by yourself?" I asked, imagining my grandfather, his knees exposed to the cold air, battling a blaze alone. I had no trouble visualizing it.

"I got the biggest part of it out before the boys came and took care of the rest of it. They made sure it was out before they left, but my truck's seen better days, that's for sure."

"Why didn't you call me sooner?" I asked him.

"I was kind of busy at the time, you know, with the fire and everything," Moose said, the weariness clearer now than it had been. It reminded me yet again that my grandfather was no longer a young man, despite what he himself believed.

"Of course," I said. "Greg and I will be there in ten minutes."

"Victoria, there's no need for you two to drag yourselves out at this time of night. I wouldn't have told you until morning, but Martha insisted that I call you as soon as the fire truck left."

"She was right," I said. "We'll see you soon."

My grandfather was still protesting as I hung up the

phone.

As I got out of bed, Greg asked me, "What's going on?"

"Go back to sleep. I'll tell you in the morning."

Instead, he got up as well. "Yeah, right. Like that's going to happen. Wherever you're going this time of night, I'm going with you."

I thanked him, and as we both hurriedly got dressed, I brought him up to speed on what had just happened.

As we were going out the door, he asked, "Should somebody call your dad?"

"I didn't even think about that," I said. "You drive, and I'll call him."

"That sounds like a plan to me," he said.

As Greg drove down the darkened streets toward my grandparents' place, I called my dad's number. I dreaded waking him up, but I knew that he'd want to know.

He was surprisingly alert when he answered my call. "Victoria?"

"Hi, Dad. Did you hear about Moose's truck?"

"Mom called me ten minutes ago. We're already on our way."

"We'll see you there, then," I said, and then I hung up.

"He already knew about it," I told Greg. "Martha called him."

"That figures," Greg said.

"What do you mean by that?" I asked, honestly curious by his statement.

"Victoria, this probably isn't the greatest time to discuss this. Let's just focus on Moose, and the fact that he's okay."

"What else do we have to talk about?" I asked.

"Well, for starters, we could discuss why someone would want to burn your grandfather's truck up. Is he sure that it wasn't a squirrel's nest or something that caught on fire by accident?"

"He seemed pretty clear that it was arson," I said. "What were you going to say about my grandmother and my dad?"

Greg let out a sigh, and then he said, "You know me; I talk

too much when I'm tired. Victoria, your grandfather and your dad are two very different men. Should it be a surprise to anyone that Martha and your dad are close?"

"I never really thought about it that way," I said.

"That's because you're so tight with Moose yourself."

"Hey, I love my father very much," I said. Why did I suddenly sound so defensive about it, though?

"Nobody knows that more than I do, but you and Moose are so much alike that it scares me sometimes. Martha can't help but see that, and neither can your father."

"You're right. I need to make more of an effort with my dad," I said.

"I'm not saying that, either. You two are plenty close. It's just in a different way. That's all that I'm saying. Listen, I didn't mean to start anything."

"You didn't," I said as I touched my husband's arm lightly. "I admit that sometimes it's an effort with my dad, but I just thought that was because he was my father, and not my grandfather."

"When this is all over, you should take your dad out to dinner or a movie, just the two of you. That's all I'm saying."

"You're not angling for a little time away from me, are you?" I asked him with an arched eyebrow. I knew that Greg could tell by my tone of voice that I was just teasing him.

"Why would I want to be away from you one more moment than I had to? You're quite delightful."

"You are, too. Thanks, Greg."

"I'm going to pretend that I know what that's for, and say you're welcome."

"I knew that there was a reason I married you," I said, my smile warm and open now.

"We're here," Greg said solemnly as he pulled into the drive away from the burned-out remnants of my grandfather's pickup truck. Contrary to what my grandfather had told me over the phone, a small fire truck was still there, and Luke Yates, our fire chief, was manning the sole remaining hose himself. My family and I were seeing a great deal of the fire chief lately, and not under the most pleasant of circumstances.

"How bad is it?" I asked as I approached him.

"I don't think he'll ever drive it again, but try telling him that. He's already called Wayne to come tow it into his shop, and the thing's barely done smoldering."

"It's not as bad as it looks," Moose said as he approached us.

"It would be hard to be worse," Greg said with a frown.

From anyone else, that comment might have gotten a stern rebuke, but Moose and my husband were close enough to tell each other the unvarnished truth most of the time. "Maybe, but if anybody can fix it, it's Wayne," Moose said.

"I agree," Greg said as my mother and father drove up.

I made it a point to greet my father first with a solid hug. "Hey, Dad."

He looked puzzled by my attention. "Victoria, is something wrong?"

My mother said, "Nothing has to be wrong for you to get a hug."

"I know that," Dad said, but from the expression on his face, it was still doubtful in his mind. He went over to his father and asked, "Are you okay?"

"Just a little soot and some smoke," Moose said. "You?"

"I'm fine," my father said, clearly a little irritated by the question. "How's your truck?"

"It might be okay," Moose said.

Dad was about to answer when Wayne drove up in his tow truck. He got out and whistled when he saw Moose's vehicle. "What happened to you? Squirrels?"

"That's what I thought," Greg said.

"No squirrel used gasoline to light my truck on fire," Moose said. After a moment's pause, he added, "Well, if one did, we have more problems than a singed truck on our hands."

"Singed? It looks downright crisp to me," Wayne said,

and then he turned to the fire chief. "Is it even safe to tow yet?"

"You should be fine," the chief said. It was clear that we weren't the only ones exhausted from this ordeal. "I wouldn't park it inside your shop just yet, though."

"There's an empty lot next to my shop," Wayne said. "Maybe I'll stick it there."

"Will it be okay?" Moose asked.

Wayne surveyed the truck again. "I think it's pretty safe to say that there's not much more harm anyone else can do to it at this point."

"You wouldn't happen to have a loaner I could drive while you look at mine, do you?" Moose asked.

"No, sorry about that." Wayne paused, frowned for a moment, and then he added reluctantly, "There *is* one old truck that's in nearly as bad a shape as this one now. You wouldn't want to drive that, would you?"

"Try me," Moose said with a grin. "I'll be by in the morning to pick it up, so don't loan it out to anybody else."

"Trust me, that's not going to be a problem. Let me load this up, and I'll see you then. You might want to call your insurance company and tell them about this, though."

"It's already been taken care of," Martha said calmly. I hadn't even noticed her approach, and when I saw my grandmother, I noticed that she was right beside my father. Maybe in some ways my husband was more observant than I was.

A thought suddenly occurred to me. "Has anyone even called the police?"

"Sheriff Croft has already been here," Moose said. "He just about beat Luke to the scene."

"Yeah, but I had to drive a fire truck," the chief said. "All he had to do was drive his squad car."

"What did he say when he saw it?" I asked Moose.

Before my grandfather answered me, he asked Wayne, "Are you ready to load it up?"

The mechanic got the hint and started attaching cables to

what was left of Moose's truck.

"That means that you don't need me anymore, either," Chief Yates said.

Moose offered a hand, which he took. "Thanks for coming."

"Just part of the service we're happy to provide," the fire chief said.

After everyone but family was gone, Moose said, "Why don't we all go inside and have a cup of coffee? Or do you folks need to get home?"

"We've got time," Dad said, and everyone else agreed.

Once we were all seated around the kitchen table and Martha had coffee brewing, I asked again, "Now that it's just family, what did the sheriff say?"

"He thought it was serious, and he warned me that we'd better stop our investigation," Moose said.

"That sounds like the most prudent course of action to me," Dad said.

"Of course it does," Moose answered.

"But we're not going to give up now, are we?" I asked my grandfather plaintively.

He grinned at me before he answered. "What do you think?"

"You're both crazy; you know that, don't you?" my dad asked.

"I don't see that they have any choice," Martha replied, surprising all of us.

"What do you mean, Mom?" my father asked her. Was there a hint of dismay in the question? He could usually take Martha's support for granted, but apparently not tonight.

"Whoever did this just made it personal. Do you think they're going to stop until they're caught, or will something much more dangerous happen to one of us next? That fire could have just as easily been in this house instead of your father's truck. Whoever did this must be caught, and they must be caught quickly."

There was a bit of stunned silence from the rest of us. Only Moose moved, patting his wife's shoulder gently. I looked at Dad, who seemed to be struggling with what his mother had just said. After a few moments, he clearly came to a decision.

"You're right." He turned to my grandfather and me and asked, "So, how do you two plan to bring this arsonist and killer to justice?"

"That's the problem," I said, voicing what I was sure that Moose was thinking as well. "At the moment, we don't have a single clue how to do it."

"Then I suggest you find one, and fast," my mother said. "In the meantime, I have to get up in a few hours, so if you'll excuse me, I'm going home to my bed."

I stood as well. "I need a little more sleep myself." I turned to Moose and asked, "Are you okay?"

"I'm as mad as a wet hornet," he said. "Does that qualify as okay?"

"I'd rather have you be mad than defeated," I said. "We'll figure this out in the morning."

Moose nodded. "You bet we will."

As we drove home, Greg asked me softly, "Do you have any ideas about catching this bad guy?"

"Not yet. Let me sleep on it," I said as I stifled a yawn.

"You only have a few hours until it's time to get up again," Greg reminded me.

"Then I'd better get to sleep as soon as possible," I said.

The truth was, I had no idea what to do next. In the past, Moose and I had mostly just followed one lead after another until we unmasked the killer, but this time it was different. It felt as though any of our three remaining suspects could be guilty, and I had no idea how to determine which one had actually killed Barry Jackson and burned down the bakery. I was fairly certain that whoever had done it had torched Moose's truck as well, most likely as a warning for us to stop digging.

The real question was who had we scared enough to make them act so boldly? From their point of view, it must have felt as though we were breathing down their necks.

From ours, we were far from that.

That meant that there was only one thing left that we could do.

The first thing tomorrow morning, or more accurately, in a few hours, Moose and I had to start stirring the pot hard and see what might come up to the surface.

If facts and interviewing techniques couldn't help us, maybe we could bluff our way into catching a killer.

Chapter 17

The next morning at the diner didn't start off that well at all. One of our earliest customers was Kenny Starnes, the town councilman who wasn't all that fond of my grandfather or me.

As he was paying his bill for breakfast, Kenny said, "Victoria, you need to be more careful. There's a spot of water on the floor near the register. You wouldn't want anyone to fall now, would you, especially if you or your grandfather were anywhere nearby. It could be fatal." He'd added the last bit loudly, trying to play to the full crowd of diners eating at The Charming Moose.

I looked for the supposed spot of water, but I couldn't see anything. "There's no water there, Kenny, and if anybody falls, it's nobody's fault but their own."

He looked sharply at me. "Is that sass you're giving me, Victoria? It's a legitimate concern."

"I'm sure it is," I said, though it was pretty clear by my tone of voice that it was nothing of the sort. "How was your breakfast?"

"As a matter of fact, it was barely edible. The eggs were undercooked, and the bacon was overdone."

I handed his ten back to him. "If you weren't satisfied with it, there's no reason at all that you should have to pay for it."

He grudgingly took the bill back. "That's decent of you."

"Honestly though, if you're that unhappy with your meal, maybe it's time to look for someplace else to have breakfast." I doubted he'd do that, since he came to the diner five mornings a week for his breakfast. Even if we lost his business, we wouldn't have to put up with seeing him anymore, which was a sacrifice that I was gladly willing to make.

Kenny must have noticed that the attention he'd gotten earlier from our other diners with his crack about falling had now backfired on him. "That won't be necessary; it's usually pretty good."

I had a brilliant idea, and I didn't stop to even think about it. "Better yet, let me get my mother out here, and you can tell her yourself about your problems with the breakfast she just made for you."

My mother was usually a mild-mannered woman, but when someone criticized her cooking, and was unjustified in doing it, she was truly fierce defending her work.

Clearly Kenny realized that himself. "On second thought, it was fine. Here, you can even keep the change." The councilman practically threw the ten at me as he hurried out the door, and once he was gone, there was a flurry of applause from my other regulars. I curtsied in thanks and then tried to get back to work. I couldn't let people like Kenny get to me. I knew that there were some folks in town who would believe the worst in me, and my grandfather, and the councilman was just feeding those bad feelings, but I didn't have to stand still and take it. It might have made more sense to ignore Kenny instead of embarrassing him, but I wasn't always known for using logic over emotion when it came to deciding my actions.

"Where's Moose?" I asked Martha when she showed up at the diner a little after nine.

"I dropped him off at Wayne's garage on the way in," she said dismissively. "I'm just glad that I don't have to ride in that wreck they are both calling a truck. If it's possible, it looks even worse than the one that's burned out. Sometimes I don't understand your grandfather at all."

I grinned at her. "Don't complain about it to me. You're the one who married him, but for the record, I'm really glad that you did."

"So am I," she said. "Usually. Don't tell him I said that."

"I'm pretty sure that he already knows."

"So, how's your morning been?" she asked me.

I shrugged. "Okay, I guess."

She took my hands in hers. "What happened, Victoria?"

"Kenny Starnes came by this morning giving me a hard time about what happened to Barry Jackson," I confessed. "I shouldn't have let him goad me, but I ended up firing right back at him."

I half expected my grandmother to chide me about my behavior, but instead, she smiled. "I'm glad to hear that. Kenny deserves to be knocked down whenever the opportunity arises."

"You're not upset with me for not turning the other cheek?" I asked.

"I applaud you. Victoria, there are some people in this world who won't back off until you smack them soundly in the nose, and Kenny Starnes is one of them."

I was about to reply when Moose came in. "Are you ready to get started, Victoria?"

"In a second," I said. "Let me tell Mom that I'm leaving first."

He nodded. "Then I have time for a cup of coffee."

"You can have breakfast, for all I care," I said. "I don't know about you, but I spent half the night trying to come up with something, but I didn't have any luck at all."

"I've got a few ideas, but they need a little more time to simmer. Breakfast sounds like a fine idea to me."

Moose found a booth, and I turned to Martha. "Why don't you join him? Ellen and I will be glad to take care of you."

"I can do it myself," Martha said as she refused to sit.

"Nonsense. At least let me serve you while I'm still here," I said.

"Come on, Martha," Moose said as he patted the seat beside him. "Let the girl wait on us if it makes her happy."

"If you're sure," Martha said as she reluctantly sat beside my grandfather.

"I'm positive," I said as I poured them each a cup of coffee. "Now, what can I get you?"

Moose pretended to study the menu, though he'd written most of it himself. After a few moments, he said, "I'll have the Big Moose breakfast with three eggs and an extra order of bacon, extra crispy." He turned to Martha and asked her, "What will you have?"

"I'll have the same thing you're having," she said with a smile.

Moose's face broke out into a huge grin. "Seriously?"

"Absolutely," she said, and then she turned to me. "Victoria, we'll both have the heart-healthy omelet and dry toast."

"Hey, that's not what I ordered at all," Moose protested.

"Maybe not, but it's what you're getting," Martha said. In a softer voice, she said, "I want you around for a long time to come, and that means you need to eat healthy."

"Fine," he said reluctantly, "but I won't be happy that I'm living longer if I can't eat whatever I want to."

"Don't be such an old bear," she said gently.

"I'm not," he replied. "Have you forgotten? I'm a moose."

"That you are," Martha said.

I went back to the kitchen and placed their orders.

Mom was frowning as I walked back. "What's wrong?"

"Why didn't you tell me what Kenny Starnes said about my breakfast? It's been two hours, Victoria, and I wouldn't have found out at all if Ellen hadn't told me."

"She shouldn't have said anything to you," I said.

"Well, it's too late for that. What was his complaint?"

"It's not important," I said, hoping Mom would drop it.

No such luck. "It might not be important to you, but it surely is to me. It's my reputation we're talking about here."

"I'm sorry. I should have told you. He said that the eggs were undercooked and the bacon was overdone."

"That's nonsense," she said. "If his food was so bad, did he leave it on the plate?"

"That thing was nearly clean enough to eat off of again," I conceded.

"The next time Mr. Town Councilman comes in here, I'll show him just how bad my cooking can be," Mom said angrily.

"He was taking a shot at Moose and me," I said. "It had nothing to do with your cooking."

"That's even worse," Mom said.

"Don't worry about it. I handled it, and I don't think that he'll be complaining again."

"He'd better not if he knows what's good for him. I have a full arsenal back here at my disposal."

"I know you do," I said. "This order is for Moose and Martha," I said as I directly handed her their order.

"Are you two hanging around the place this morning?" Mom asked as she got started on their meals.

"We're regrouping," I said as I nodded.

"Is that a fancy way of saying that you're stumped?" Mom asked with a smile.

"Pretty much," I admitted.

"Don't worry. You'll figure something out. You always do."

"I hope you're right," I said, and then I got back to my tables. I needn't have bothered. Ellen had everything under control.

I stopped by the booth where Moose and Martha were sitting. "It'll just be a minute."

"I can hardly wait," Moose said deadpan.

"You'll enjoy it, and you know it," Martha said.

"Well, I will say this. If anyone can make it edible, it will be Melinda." He turned to me and said, "Victoria, your mother doesn't get nearly enough credit for being as good as she is behind the grill."

"I agree," I said. "Would you say that she's as good as you are?"

"Well," Moose said, drawing the word out.

"I'm just teasing. I like to think that you, Greg, and Mom all have equally impressive skills cooking here."

"That's a diplomatic way to put it," Martha said with a smile.

"It has the benefit of being true, too," I said as their order appeared in the window. "I'll be right back."

I retrieved their food and delivered it. Moose stared at his healthy omelet for a few seconds, and Martha prodded him with her elbow. "Go on. Take a bite. It's good."

"I'm sure that it is. What it's not, though, is a double order of bacon."

Martha laughed. "Agreed. It's also not a heart attack waiting to happen."

Moose took a forkful of the omelet and tasted it. "That's not bad," he said.

"I'll be sure to pass your compliments on to the chef," I said.

"Tell her I said that it was delightful, then," Moose said.

After they ate, Martha stood and started bussing their table.

"I can do that myself," I said.

"Nonsense. You two need to get going and solve this murder."

"Come on, Victoria," Moose said as he stood. "I learned a long time ago that there was no sense arguing with Martha about anything."

"If only that were true," my grandmother said with a smile.

"Besides, I haven't seen your new truck," I said, joking.

"Don't give him any ideas, Victoria. It's just a loaner."

"The girl has a point, Martha. What if Wayne can't get my old truck back on the road? This could be an answer to all of our problems."

"Moose Nelson, if you think I'm going anywhere with you in that rattling death trap, then you're sadly mistaken. You can afford to buy a new truck, so why don't you?"

Moose frowned. "New trucks don't have the personality that the old ones have."

"Not if you call rust and patches of paint personality," Martha said.

"You'll see. She'll grow on you."

"If she does, I'll have my doctor remove her," Martha said.

"Come on, Victoria," my grandfather said. "Let's go someplace that my fine transportation is appreciated for what it is." He winked at my grandmother as we left, and I offered her a wink myself.

She winked back, and I thought it was just for me, but to be fair, Moose probably thought the exact same thing.

"So, what are these brilliant ideas of yours?" I asked Moose as we walked out of the diner. "Hang on a second. Is that it?" I pointed to a beat-up old truck that looked as though it had to be towed everywhere it went. The driver's side door panel was bright orange, while most of the rest of the truck's body was painted in gray primer, at least the parts that weren't covered in open rust. The hood looked as though a tree had fallen on it at some point, and the tailgate was being held on with bungee cords. "Do I need a tetanus shot before I climb into that thing?"

"Take my word for it; she's sturdier than she looks," Moose said.

"She'd have to be, wouldn't she? Maybe I should drive my car."

My grandfather shook his head. "I'm driving, Victoria. Think of it this way. No one will know that it's us in this truck."

"I surely hope not," I said. I tugged on the passenger side door to no avail. "I can't get it to open."

"Wayne warned me that it sticks sometimes," he said. "Let me see if I can get it." My grandfather tried the door, but it wouldn't open for him, either. He then pounded on it a few times, harder and harder each time. After a few tries, it finally opened, creaking with the sound of metal on metal as it finally swung open, though only part of the way.

"Go on and get in," Moose said. "I'll close it behind you."

"I've got a hunch that you're going to have to," I said.

Once I was inside, I saw that the cracked vinyl bench seat had more duct tape on it than original material. At least there was a seat belt.

After I latched it, Moose put some real muscle into closing my door, finally succeeding, and I prayed that I didn't have to get out in a hurry.

Once my grandfather was settled in beside me, he looked quite satisfied. "There you go. That wasn't so bad, now was it?"

"Compared to what?" I asked as he started the engine. I had to give the mechanic credit. Wayne had the old beast purring, which was quite a bit better than I'd imagined when I'd first seen it.

"Listen to that. The engine sounds great."

"It does," I agreed. "But there's only one problem."

"Just one?" my grandfather asked as he grinned at me.

"So far, anyway."

"What is it, then?"

"We don't know what we're going to do next," I explained.

"Don't worry. I've got a plan."

"Well, if you don't mind, I'd love to hear it," I said.

That's when Moose started to explain his idea to me.

"I think I've figured out a way to use what happened to my truck last night to our advantage," my grandfather said.

"Go on. I'm listening."

"What if we tell our suspects that one of my security cameras at the house picked up an image of the person who committed the arson?"

"Moose, you don't have security cameras," I reminded him.

"Not right now, but I will in half an hour. I've got a guy who's putting some in for me right now."

"Isn't that kind of locking the barn door after the horse is gone?"

"Victoria, how's the arsonist going to know that those cameras haven't been in place all along?" my grandfather asked.

"They won't," I said, "but if there was anything to see, we

wouldn't have to bluff our suspects."

He smiled. "I've already thought of a solution to that. We're going to tell our suspects the same story. There's an image on the DVD I record my security on, but it needs to be enhanced. We have someone coming over tonight to look at it, because we can't tell the sheriff what we have until we have a positive ID."

"It sounds complicated," I said.

"Does that mean you don't think it will work?" Moose asked.

"No, I think it's worth a shot," I agreed. "You don't want a killer breaking into your house looking for that DVD, though, do you?"

"I hadn't thought of that," Moose acknowledged.

"Let's say that the equipment is all in your garden shed," I said. "That way it will be easier to watch from the house." Moose had built a small shed for his garden tools years ago, but who was to say that it didn't now house video surveillance equipment as well?

"That works for me. We might as well try it. After all, what have we got to lose?"

"I can think of a ton of things right off the top of my head," I said with a smile, "but that's never stopped us before. Can your friend drop off an old DVD recorder and put some phony cables up inside the shed, too?"

"Let me call him and see," Moose said. After a minute, he hung up with a grin. "We're all set. By the time we tell our first suspect the plan, the trap will be set."

"Then let's get started," I said. "I'm ready to catch a killer. How about you?"

"Don't forget that I want revenge for what happened to my truck, too," Moose said.

"That's just going to be a big fat bonus when we catch our bad guy," I said.

We paid our first visit to Mike Jackson.

He greeted us at the door with less than a cordial

welcome.

"What are you two doing here?" he asked sullenly.

"We just wanted to let you know that we've just about caught our killer," Moose said.

That got Mike's attention. "How did you manage to do that?"

Moose explained his trap, and the murder victim's brother looked a little troubled by my grandfather's explanation. "What makes you think you'll be able to identify the arsonist if you can't see who it is now?"

"My friend has some specialized equipment that can light the dark up like it's daytime."

"You know, whoever torched your truck might not have killed Barry," Mike said.

"What are the odds of that? It would be too much of a coincidence otherwise," I said.

"Maybe so. Well, good luck. I have to get back to work."

After we left his place, I asked Moose, "What do you think?"

"Too soon to say," my grandfather replied. "Let's move on to Sandy."

We found her waiting tables, but she was due for a break, and she reluctantly agreed to spend part of it talking to us.

Before Moose could tell her his cover story, she said, "Sorry to hear about your truck."

"How did you know about that already?" he asked her.

"The fire chief came by this morning, and I overheard him talking about it."

"Well, it might not have been in vain," my grandfather said, and then he told her the story we'd agreed on.

"I don't know," Sandy said. "It sounds kind of iffy to me."

"My friend is confident that once he works his magic tonight, we'll be able to see who burned up my truck."

"Maybe," Sandy said, and then she glanced at her watch.

"Listen, my break is almost over. I have to get back to work."

"That was less than a spectacular result, too," I said as we headed to the business where our last suspect was.

"I know," Moose said with a frown. "No one seems all that interested in our story. This might just turn out to be one big bust after all."

"At least we've got one more trap to set. Who knows? Maybe this one will be the winner."

It wasn't.

Rob Bester barely spoke three words to us before he dismissed us out of hand. He was too busy to be bothered with our promises that the killer would soon be caught, and he barely took the time to listen to the details of our elaborate plan before he walked off.

"What now?" I asked my grandfather. It was clear that the idea, though not without merit, had pretty much failed to arouse anyone's sense of guilt, suspicion, or fear of being caught.

"What do you think? We need to go to my place and start watching that garden shed. At least we'll be able to do it from the kitchen table. It's about as comfortable a place to sit and watch for hours that I can think of."

"How long do we give it?" I asked.

"At least four hours," Moose said as he glanced at his watch, "or until we catch someone."

An hour later, it didn't seem to matter anymore.

I answered my phone, and Sheriff Croft identified himself immediately. He sounded triumphant as he explained, "Just thought you should know. We got him."

"Who are you talking about?" I asked him.

"Mike Jackson," he answered. "Something must have spooked him today, because he drained Barry's account and then tried to take off. After one of my officers caught him speeding, we got a warrant and searched his house and his garage."

"Did you have any luck?"

"Absolutely. We found two identical cans of gasoline that were used in the bakery fire, and both of them were full to the top. At least he didn't get a chance to use those, too. I wonder why he ran?"

"Maybe Moose and I had something to do with that," I said.

"What are you talking about, Victoria?"

I explained our plan to him, and after a moment or two, the sheriff said, "That's not bad. It looks like you made him run."

"When did you catch him?" I asked.

"Just a few minutes ago, as a matter of fact."

"Has he confessed to killing his brother and torching the bakery?" I asked.

"No, he's demanding to see a lawyer. He won't say a word to us," the sheriff said.

"That doesn't necessarily mean that he's guilty, though."

"Why else would he run?"

"I don't know. You're probably right," I said.

"Trust me, he did it, and it's just going to be a matter of time before we can prove it. In the meantime, we're holding him on the speeding violation. You and your grandfather helped out a lot on this case, Victoria."

"It doesn't feel like we did much of anything," I admitted.

"You found the main source of evidence, and you goaded the killer into panicking. That sounds like an awful lot to me. Maybe you didn't participate in the arrest, but you can't have everything. At least now you should sleep better at night."

"Thanks for calling," I said.

"I just thought you had a right to know," he said. "I'm going into the interrogation room right now, so my phone will be turned off, just so you know."

After I caught Moose up on what the sheriff had told me, I asked him, "What do you think? Did Mike really kill his own brother for money?"

"It sure sounds like it," Moose said as he stood and stretched. "I guess we should get you back to work so I can collect my wife."

"I guess we should," I said.

I walked out the door to Moose's truck, with my grandfather right behind me.

We didn't make it, though.

"Stop right where you are. I'm going to need that DVD before your friend sees it," the killer said as he pointed a gun at my grandfather and me, and I wondered if this was going to be the end of us.

Chapter 18

"Take it easy, Rob," Moose said as he glanced over at me. "There's no need to do anything rash."

"You know what? You don't get to tell me to do anything, Moose," Rob said. "I can't afford to have you show that evidence to the police. I'm just glad that it wasn't being digitally recorded. I would be in jail by now if it were."

I was about to confess that there wasn't a DVD, but Moose answered before I could. "It's in the garden shed," he said. "Let me go get it for you."

Moose took a step toward the shed when Rob said, "Stop right where you are, unless you want me to shoot your precious granddaughter."

That got Moose's attention, and he stopped dead in his tracks. "I'm not going anywhere. Listen, without the DVD, we don't have any proof that you torched my truck, or killed Barry Jackson. Once you have that, there's no need to kill anybody else."

"What am I supposed to do, take your word for that?" Rob asked. "If Mike finds out that I'm the one who killed his brother, he'll never sell the lot to me."

"Mike's in jail right now himself," I blurted out.

Rob looked at me. "Mike? Why?"

"The police think that he killed Barry, not you," I said.

Rob frowned. "That was a backup plan that I was hoping that I wouldn't have to use."

Moose asked him, "What good did it do for you to frame Mike if you needed him to sell you that land? You clearly didn't think this through, did you?"

"The cops weren't meant to find that gasoline," Rob said. "I just wanted to show Mike that if he didn't behave, he might be next."

"Behave in what way?" I asked.

"That was the beauty of it all," Rob said, clearly admiring his own work. "He still doesn't know that I'm behind everything that's been happening lately. I suppose they got the note, too?"

"What note are you talking about?" I asked.

"Don't worry, they'll find it soon enough," Rob said.

"Why don't you enlighten us?" Moose asked as I saw him take a slow step toward Rob.

"Sure, why not? What can it hurt at this point? I sent Mike a note, anonymously of course, that the killer was watching him, so he'd better do as he was told, or he'd pay the same price that his brother had."

"Wouldn't that tell him that you were the one who did it?" I asked.

"Selling the land to me wasn't the only thing on the list of demands. I told him that he had to pay Cliff back what his brother owed him, and find a way to help Sandy get over his brother, or he'd die the same way."

"Cliff hasn't been a suspect in the police's eyes for quite a while," I said.

Rob shrugged. "Who cares? It was just meant to divert suspicion away from me, and evidently it worked."

"Is that why Mike ran today?" I asked.

"Probably," Rob said with a chuckle. "After he got my note and found the gas cans in his garage, I can't really blame him for panicking, though I should have seen that coming. I was threatening him, plain and simple. I never thought about making him my scapegoat, but I like it. If he's convicted, that land will be auctioned off, so I'll just buy it then."

"How do we fit into your little plan?" I asked. "I've spoken with the sheriff about him arresting Mike, so he'll know that Barry's brother didn't kill us."

Rob frowned. "Who's to say that he didn't have an accomplice?"

"Like you?" Moose asked. "Is that really smart?"

"Stop saying that!" Rob was clearly getting rattled by

Moose's comments. Was my grandfather just being ornery, or was there method to his madness? Maybe if he got Rob upset, he wouldn't think straight, and we could use it to our advantage.

Then again, it might get us both killed sooner, and in much worse ways.

I wasn't thrilled with the gamble that my grandfather was taking, but now that he had, I had to back him one hundred percent. "He's right, Rob," I said, adding a little twist to my own words. "Nobody with any sense at all would hurt us now. If you let us go, it's your word against ours, but if you do something to either one of us, the law is going to come crashing down on you like a house made of stone."

He didn't like that. "Shut up, Victoria! I need to think!"

Moose wouldn't let up, though. "How long do you think you've got before someone sees us together out here? The clock's ticking, Robbie Boy. You'd better make up your mind quickly."

Rob Bester looked wildly around, and I thought about jumping at him since I was closer, but Moose must have had the same idea. As my grandfather started to move, Rob lashed out and grabbed my arm, jerking me closer to the gun he was holding in his other hand. "Don't do it, Moose! I'm warning you!"

My grandfather held his hands up high in the air. "I'm not doing a thing, Rob. Just let the girl go. That's all that I ask."

He didn't though, and instead pulled me closer to him. "Do you want to die today, Moose?"

"No, not particularly," my grandfather admitted.

"Let me ask you something, then. Which would be worse, me putting a bullet in you, or your granddaughter?"

"I've got an idea. Why don't you shoot me and leave her alone," my grandfather said without hesitation. I hoped with all of my heart that it didn't come to that, but I was proud of his request nonetheless.

"How about if you don't shoot anybody," I said. "Let me go get the DVD for you, and then you can decide."

"You're staying right where you are," Rob said as he jammed the gun into my ribs.

"Ow, that hurt!" I said.

"It's going to hurt a lot more if I pull the trigger," Rob said. "Moose, you go get it. I'm warning you. If you try anything funny, she's going to die before you can ever get to me."

"I won't do anything but what you ask," Moose said woodenly. It sounded as though my grandfather had lost his fighting spirit with my life in jeopardy.

I wasn't about to give up, though.

I stared at my grandfather as he looked my way, and I nodded slightly, blinking as I did so. I just hoped he realized that I was telling him not to waste this opportunity to fight back. Sure, I might die in the process, but there was a possibility that at least he could get away. If he gave Rob the dummy DVD, we were both dead, so why not take a chance that at least one of us might live through this?

Moose started to go into the garden shed when Rob stopped him. "Not so fast. Take out your cell phone, and put it on the ground."

"What makes you think I have one on me?" Moose asked.

Rob jabbed me harder in the ribs, a move that caught me by surprise. I gasped as it dug in, and without another word, Moose pulled out his phone and did as he was told.

"Good boy," Rob said. "Now smash it with your foot."

Moose frowned for a moment, but he did as he was told, and the phone was rendered useless.

"Now go do what you're supposed to, and nothing more," the killer commanded. It was clear that he was enjoying ordering us around.

As Moose disappeared inside, I asked Rob, "Why the hard push for Barry's land, anyway? Do you want to expand so much that you'd kill for the opportunity?"

"You still don't get it, do you?"

"Tell me," I said, hoping to distract him enough for Moose to make his play.

"*None* of it was my idea," Rob said, spitting the words out as though they caused him pain. "From the beginning, good old Cliff has been pulling my strings."

"What?" I asked, clearly surprised by the statement despite my predicament.

"You and your crime-solving grandfather didn't think of that, did you?"

"If Cliff wanted Barry to sell you the land, why didn't he just make him do it?"

"He tried," Rob said, "but Barry wouldn't follow instructions. Cliff got tough with him, and when I found Barry in the bakery that morning, he was already beaten up pretty thoroughly."

"But he wasn't dead yet, was he?" I asked.

"Who can say that he wouldn't have died eventually from the beating? I just sped things along, that's all. Barry was never going to cave in to Cliff, and I needed the loan shark off my back. The only way I was going to do that was to take care of Barry myself."

"Why the fire, though?" Had Moose frozen in the shed trying to decide what to do next? No, knowing my grandfather, he was still trying to come up with a plan to save us both.

I just hoped that he hurried.

"What better way to torch a bakery? I was going to burn the place to the ground to change Barry's mind, but when I found him inside, he was barely able to hold his own head up after the beating he took. In the end, it just seemed like too good an opportunity to pass up."

"And you did that all because Cliff told you to?" I asked. What was keeping Moose? I was running out of ways to distract Rob short of directly attacking him, and that wasn't really an option, given the fact that he was holding the gun on me.

"Why wouldn't I? We'd be square then, and I could go back to running my own life. Moose was right, by the way. I was just bluffing about my grandfather leaving me any money. It was going to be Cliff's cash all along. He was going to use my operation as some kind of drug distribution center." Evidently Rob had had enough of waiting for my grandfather, and my distractions hadn't worked after all. He called out loudly, "Moose, you've got ten seconds to come out with that DVD, or I'm shooting Victoria, and then I'm coming in after it myself."

"I'm right here," Moose said as he emerged from the shed. He was cupping the DVD in his hand in an odd way, keeping it flat as though it were some sort of offering. As far as I could see, there were no weapons anywhere on him.

It appeared that the counterattack was going to be up to me.

I braced myself to move quickly, knowing that Rob would have to pull the gun from my side or release me to take the DVD from Moose.

Either way, we still had a chance, but I had to time it perfectly.

Moose got within two steps of us both, and I noticed that something was on top of the DVD.

Before Rob could see it, I jerked a little, bringing his attention back to me.

"Stop squirming, Victoria," he said as he looked over at me, easing his grip just a little bit.

Moose acted then, blowing the substance on top of the DVD directly into Rob's face. The killer screamed as he clawed at his eyes with one hand, the gun still clutched in the other, and I jerked away from him as I stomped down on his foot. I was wearing tennis shoes, but it still caught him off guard, and he finally dropped the gun.

I went for it, but not before Moose knocked me away and got it himself.

"Get down on the ground, Rob," Moose ordered.

"The lye blinded me! My eyes are on fire!" he said, whimpering in pain.

"Victoria, get him some water," Moose ordered. "There's a bucket by the shed."

I started to go toward the water when I heard something behind me.

Evidently Rob wasn't nearly as blind as he'd claimed to be.

When I looked back, I saw my grandfather and him locked in combat for control of the gun. While Moose was as strong as most men in their prime, Rob was evidently a little stronger.

And the bad guy was clearly winning.

Rushing over and reaching inside the shed, I pulled out a pitchfork, the first thing I could get my hands on. Racing back to the men, I circled around to get a clear strike at Rob when he finally wrestled the gun out of my grandfather's hands.

The look of triumph on his face lasted only an instant as I stabbed him with the pitchfork, embedding it directly into the arm that had just moments ago been holding a gun.

Rob screamed in pain as he dropped the gun and tried to free his arm from the garden-tool-turned-weapon, and I picked the handgun up and pointed it straight at his heart.

"Pull it out!" he screamed as he tried to pry the pitchfork out with his good hand.

Moose started to move forward, but I put a hand on his arm.

"He's not faking this time, Victoria," my grandfather said.

"I don't care. It's not going to kill him. Leave it in, and the police can pull it out for him." I handed him my cell phone and said, "Call Sheriff Croft."

There must have been something in my voice that told Moose the best thing he could do was to obey my wishes. At that moment, thinking about what Rob had been capable of doing to me and my family, I didn't mind him suffering a little bit of pain at all.

He'd live, which was more than I could say for us if he'd gotten his way.

Chapter 19

"I don't believe I've ever seen a pitchfork used as a weapon before," the sheriff said after they took Rob Bester away in the ambulance. The paramedics had been afraid to remove it themselves, so they'd transported the killer with it still stuck in his arm, though it made for a tight fit in the ambulance.

"By the way, we're going to need that pitchfork back," Moose said.

Sheriff Croft nodded. "I'll make a note of it." He actually jotted something down in his notebook, whether it was pitchfork-related or not I couldn't say.

"It sounds as though all Mike Jackson is guilty of is being gullible," the sheriff said. "When he ran, I thought for sure that he was our man."

"It was a natural enough thing to believe," I said. It was easy to be magnanimous now that Moose and I had cornered the real killer.

"You weren't fooled, though," the sheriff said.

"She might not have been, but I was," Moose said.

"That's kind of you to say," Sheriff Croft said.

"What kills me is that Cliff is going to get away free and clear, even though his actions behind the scenes caused this whole mess in the first place."

"Don't worry about Cliff," the sheriff said. "Do you remember the alibi he had for Barry's murder?"

"You said that the police in Charlotte had him under surveillance," I said.

"Well, they caught him doing something nearly as bad as committing murder, so he's not exactly walking away from this unscathed. Unless I miss my guess, he's going to jail for a long time. Maybe they'll even put Rob in the cell with him. That would be interesting, wouldn't it?"

"Now that they're both out of my life, I don't care what happens to them," I said. "The person I feel most sorry for besides Barry is Sandy Hardesty. She might not be my favorite person in the world, but she lost someone she cared about through no fault of her own."

"I wouldn't worry about Sandy," the sheriff said. "I saw her this afternoon flirting with Luke Yates."

"He's old enough to be her father," I said.

"Grandfather," Moose corrected me, "but that doesn't mean anything these days."

"Are you telling me that if something happened to Martha you'd go find yourself a girl younger than me?" I asked him.

"Victoria, believe me when I say that as much as I love your grandmother, if something were ever to happen to her, that would be the end of it for me."

"That's better," I said, though I wasn't sure that I completely believed him.

"Well, if you two will excuse me, I've got work to do," Sheriff Croft said. "We'll need statements from both of you, but that can wait until morning if you'd like."

"It's early yet," I said. "If it's all the same to you, I'd just as soon get it over with right now."

"That sounds like a plan to me," the sheriff said as Greg drove up. Martha was in the front seat with him, and Mom and Dad were riding in back.

"We'll all be there," Moose said.

"I figured as much," the sheriff replied as he shook his head gently. "See you all soon."

As Sheriff Croft drove off, our family collected Moose and me in a family embrace. Four sets of questions hit us as my grandfather and I tried to answer everyone at once, but I didn't mind it one bit.

I was happy for the chaos, and being a member of a family where there was so much love.

As we all crammed into Greg's car and drove to the police station together, I felt bad for Mike Jackson.

He'd lost the last bit of family he'd had, and from now on, he'd be going it all alone, with no one else to share old memories with.

It was, in its own way, a death sentence to his past, and I was happy that mine would never suffer that fate, not unless I lived a very, very long time.

Topless Chicken Surprise

This simple yet delightful recipe became a staple in my household one day when I just didn't feel like making the crust for my standard chicken potpie. When my family asked me what the meal was called, I came up with the name off the top of my head, and of course, it stuck! This is what I think of as the epitome of hearty diner fare, with all of the homey scents and flavors of a meal that Mom could have served herself.

This meal goes great with mashed potatoes, green beans, and a side of cranberry sauce. If I'm feeling really adventurous, I add stuffing as well. I used to make my own, but the stovetop varieties are so good now that I skip the work and make it instead. No one in my family has complained yet about the substitution. Toast or biscuits also work nicely with this.

Ingredients

1 large packet (about 2 cups) frozen vegetables, your choice (I like the peas, carrots, and green beans)
2 whole chicken breasts, broiled or boiled, pulled or cut into bite-size pieces

Sauce
This is my recipe for a simple white sauce. If you'd like to convert it to a cheese sauce, just add a cup of shredded cheddar cheese at the end, but I wouldn't recommend doing it for this meal!

6 tablespoons butter,
6 tablespoons all-purpose flour
1½ cups of whole, 2%, or 1% milk; the richer the better,

though
salt and pepper to taste

Directions

Heat the vegetable pack in the microwave per the package directions, and make sure your cooked chicken is warmed throughout if you've made it ahead of time and kept it refrigerated. Set these ingredients aside and start on the next step.

Melt the butter in a large skillet on the stovetop at low heat. Once the butter is melted, take the skillet off the heat and slowly add the flour, along with a few dashes of salt and pepper. Stir the mixture thoroughly, then return it to low heat. Continue stirring until the flour is completely incorporated, which takes about a minute.

Next, add about 1/4 of the milk, stirring until the mixture begins to come together. There shouldn't be any clumps at this point, giving you a smooth, velvety texture throughout. Next, add the remainder of the milk and turn the heat to high. Now is the time to be vigilant, stirring the mixture constantly as it works toward a boil. When the first bubble appears, remove the skillet from the heat and continue stirring for thirty seconds.

Add the chicken and vegetables to the gravy you've just created, stirring it all in to make sure that everything is coated.

The meal is now ready to serve along with the sides you've created.

Enjoy!

Feeds 3–5 people, depending on their appetites!

If you enjoy Jessica Beck Mysteries and you would like to be notified when the next book is being released, please send your email address to newreleases@jessicabeckmysteries.net. Your email address will not be shared, sold, bartered, traded, broadcast, or disclosed in any way. There will be no spam from us, just a friendly reminder when the latest book is being released.

Also, be sure to visit our website at jessicabeckmysteries.net for valuable information about Jessica's books.

Made in the USA
San Bernardino, CA
21 August 2014